REASONABLE DOUBTS

Gianrico Carofiglio

Translated from the Italian
by Howard Curtis

T0162053

BITTER LEMON PRESS
LONDON

BITTER LEMON PRESS

New edition 2012
First published in the United Kingdom in 2007 by
Bitter Lemon Press, 37 Arundel Gardens, London W11 2LW

www.bitterlemonpress.com

First published in Italian as *Ragionevoli dubbi* by
Sellerio editore, Palermo, 2006

Bitter Lemon Press gratefully acknowledges the financial
assistance of the Arts Council of England.

A CIP record for this book is available from the
British Library

ISBN 978-1-904738-541

Printed and bound by
CPI Group (UK) Ltd, Croydon, CR0 4YY

Award-winning, best-selling Italian crime novelist Gianrico Carofiglio is the author of three other novels featuring the character of defence lawyer Guido Guerrieri: *Involuntary Witness*, *A Walk in the Dark* and *Temporary Perfections*. A former prosecutor in Bari, Puglia, Carofiglio is an expert in the investigation of organized crime and related psychology. Carofiglio's books have been translated into seventeen languages worldwide.

Reasonable Doubts

0

When Margherita said she wanted to talk to me, I thought she was going to tell me she was expecting a baby.

It was late on a September afternoon. The sky had that dramatic end-of-summer light that gives a foretaste of the gloom and mystery of autumn. A good time to find out I'm going to be a father, I clearly remember thinking as we sat down on the terrace, with the low sun behind us.

"I've been offered a new job. A very good one. But if I accept, I have to go away for several months. Maybe a year."

I looked at her, puzzled, like someone who either hasn't quite heard, or hasn't understood what he has heard. What did this offer of work have to do with the child we'd be having in a few months? I couldn't figure it out.

She explained. A major American advertising agency – she even told me the name, but I forgot it immediately, maybe wasn't even listening – had offered her the job of coordinating the campaign for the relaunch of an airline company. She mentioned a name, a very big name, and said it was a once-in-a-lifetime opportunity.

A once-in-a-lifetime opportunity. I let the words bounce around my head. They were painful, like the dull throb of a migraine. It suddenly seemed to me as if the meaning of everything revolved around some invisible point that I couldn't locate or define.

"When did you get this offer?"

"In July. We were in contact a few times before then, but they made the formal offer in July."

"*Before we went on holiday,*" I said, *as if it was important.*

But maybe it really was.

Then I realized. If she was telling me now, in September, two months after receiving the offer, and God knows how long after they first made contact, that meant she had already made up her mind, maybe even said yes.

"*You've already said yes.*"

"*No. I wanted to tell you first.*"

"*You've made up your mind.*"

She hesitated briefly – the only time she did – then nodded.

I'd been thinking she was about to tell me she was expecting a baby. I'd been thinking that at the age of forty-two my insipid life was suddenly, as if by magic, about to have a meaning, a reason. All because of that boy, or girl, I'd be able to teach a few things before I got too old.

I didn't say that. I kept it all inside, like something you feel ashamed to even be thinking. Because you're ashamed of your own weakness, your own fragility.

Instead, I asked her when she'd be leaving, and I must have seemed ridiculously calm, because she looked at me with a mixture of surprise and anxiety. From the street came the angry, prolonged snarl of a moped with a souped-up exhaust. I'd remember that sound, I thought. I'd hear it again every time that unexpected, pitiless scene came back into my mind.

She didn't know when she'd be leaving. Ten days, two weeks. But she definitely had to be in Milan by the end of the month, and in New York by the middle of October.

So, I thought, she did know when she was leaving after all.

We were silent for two or three minutes. Or more.

"*Don't you want to know why?*"

No, I didn't want to know why. Or maybe I did, but I said no all the same. I didn't want her to burden me with her reasons – which I was sure were excellent reasons – to ease her heart, or her soul, or wherever

2

it is our guilt is located. I had my own guilt, and she had hers. I would think about it in the weeks and months to come, tormenting myself with that question and the memories and all the rest of it.

But for that tepid, pitiless September afternoon, we'd said enough.

I stood up and said I was going back to my apartment, or maybe going out.

"Guido, don't do this to me. Say something, I beg you."

But I didn't say anything. I didn't know what to say.

"I'm not going for ever. If you do this, you'll make me feel like a worm."

She had no sooner said these words than she regretted them. Maybe she saw the lost look on my face, or maybe she simply realized it wasn't right. It may have been inevitable – she must have been thinking about it for a good many weeks – but it certainly wasn't right.

She said some other things, too, her voice breaking. They sounded like apologies. Which is what they were.

And as she said these things I stopped listening to her, and the whole scene took on the unreal texture of a photographic negative, and that was the way it lodged itself in my memory.

1

I was waiting for the judges to enter the courtroom and my case to be heard, when I noticed a young woman sitting on the public benches. Oriental, but with something European about her features. She looked beautiful and slightly bewildered.

I wondered who she was there for, and several times I pretended to search for something on my bench so that I could turn and look at her.

I had the impression she was watching me, which was of course highly unlikely. A girl like that would never have given me the time of day, I thought, not even in the good old days. Then I thought, when the hell were the good old days anyway?

At least ten minutes passed like this. Then at last the judges emerged from their chamber, the hearing started, and I stopped having these stupid thoughts.

*

It was a trial for armed robbery and we were due to hear the principal witness: the victim. A jewel salesman who'd had his sample case stolen, along with the unused gun he carried with him.

Two of the robbers had been arrested soon after the crime, with the booty still in their car. They had opted for the fast-track procedure and had already received relatively light sentences. My client was accused of being the lookout.

4

The victim had recognized him from a photograph album at police headquarters. The trial was being held *in absentia* because my client – Signor Albanese, amateur footballer and professional criminal – had run away when he had found out they were looking for him. He'd only just finished a prison term and had no desire to go back inside. And he said he had nothing to do with this case.

The assistant prosecutor's examination of the witness didn't take long. The jewel salesman looked very determined and not at all intimidated by his surroundings. He confirmed everything he had already told the police, confirmed that he had recognized my client from a photograph, the photograph was admitted in evidence, and the presiding judge asked me to proceed with my cross-examination.

"You have stated that the robbery was committed by three men. Two of them physically snatched the sample case and the gun from you, while the third was standing some distance away and seemed to be the lookout. Is that correct?"

"Yes. The third man was on the corner, but then the three of them all left together."

"And is it also correct that the third man, the one you later identified from a photograph, was standing about twenty yards away from you?"

"Fifteen or twenty yards."

"I see. Now I'd like you to tell us briefly how you came to recognize the photo at police headquarters, the day after the robbery."

"They gave me some albums to look at and one of them had the photo of the man in it."

"Had you ever seen him before? I mean, before the robbery?"

"No. But when I saw his face in the album, I immediately

thought: I know this man. And then I realized it was the one who'd been the lookout."

"Do you play football?"

"I'm sorry?"

"I asked you if you play football."

The presiding judge asked me what relevance this question had to the matter in hand. I assured him that everything would become clear in the next few minutes and he told me to go ahead.

"Do you play football? Do you take part in any championships?"

He said he did. I took a photo of two football teams out of my file, the kind of photo that's taken before matches. I asked the presiding judge for permission to approach the witness and show him the photo.

"Do you recognize anyone in this photograph?"

"Of course. That's me, and these are the others in my team . . ."

"Could you tell us when it was taken?"

"Last summer, at the championship finals."

"Do you remember the date?"

"I think it was the twentieth or twenty-first of August."

"About a month before the robbery?"

"I think so, yes."

"Did you know the people on the other team?"

"Some of them, not all."

"Would you please look at the photo again and tell me if you recognize anyone from the other team?"

He took the photo and examined it closely, running his index finger over the faces of the players. "I know this one, but I don't know his name. I think this one is called Pasquale . . . I don't remember his surname. This one . . ."

His expression changed. He looked at me in surprise, then looked at the photo again.

"Do you recognize anyone else?"

"This one . . . looks like . . ."

"Who does he look like?"

"He looks a bit like that photo . . ."

"Do you mean the one you recognized in the album at police headquarters?"

"He looks a bit like him. It's hard to —"

"It is in fact the same person. Do you remember him now?"

"Yes, it could be him."

"Now that you've remembered him, can you state that the person who played football against your team that evening in August was the same person who took part in the robbery?"

". . . I'm not so sure now . . . It's hard to say after so much time."

"Of course, I realize that. Let me put it another way. When you were robbed and you saw the third man some twenty yards away, did you realize it might be the same person you'd played football against a month earlier?"

"No, how could I? . . . It was a long way away . . ."

"Precisely, it was a long way away. Thank you, Your Honour, I've finished."

The presiding judge read out the date for the next hearing and as he was telling the bailiff to call another case I turned to look for the Oriental girl. It took a few seconds, because she was no longer where I had seen her at the beginning of the hearing. She was standing very close to the exit, about to leave.

Our eyes met for a few moments. Then she turned and disappeared into the corridors of the courthouse.

2

The telegram arrived two days later. The wording is always more or less the same.

The prisoner, Mr So-and-so, appoints you as his defence counsel, states the number assigned for his court appearance, and asks you to visit him in prison to discuss his situation.

In this case the prisoner's name was Fabio Paolicelli, he stated the number assigned for his court appearance, and asked me to visit him in prison *urgently*.

Fabio Paolicelli. Who was he? The name sounded vaguely familiar, but I couldn't quite place it. And that bothered me because I'd become convinced lately that I was getting worse at remembering names. I took it as a worrying sign that my mental faculties were deteriorating. Bullshit, of course – I've never been good at remembering names, and I had exactly the same problem when I was twenty. But once you're past forty you start to think all kinds of stupid things, and quite insignificant phenomena become symptoms of impending old age.

Anyway, I racked my brains for a few minutes and then gave up. I'd find out if I really knew the guy soon enough, when I went to see him in prison.

I called Maria Teresa and asked her if we had any appointments for the afternoon. She told me we were waiting for Signor Abbaticchio, but that he'd be coming late, just before we closed.

So, seeing as it was four o'clock on a Thursday, and seeing as it's possible to visit clients in prison until six o'clock on Thursdays, and especially seeing as I didn't feel in the mood to start studying the files for the following day's hearings, I decided to make the acquaintance of Signor Fabio Paolicelli, who wanted to see me *urgently*. That way, the afternoon wouldn't be wasted. Not completely, anyway.

For some months now, I'd been riding a bicycle. Since Margherita had left I'd made a few changes in my life. I didn't really know why, but making these changes had helped me. Among them was the purchase of a nice, old-fashioned black bicycle, without gears, which would have been no use in the streets of Bari anyway. To cut a long story short, I'd stopped using my car and I liked it. I'd started by cycling to the courthouse, then I'd taken to cycling to the prison, which is further, and in the end I'd even stopped using the car to go out in the evenings, seeing as usually, wherever I went, I went alone.

It can be dangerous going around Bari by bike: there are no bicycle lanes, and motorists regard you as nothing more than a nuisance. But you get everywhere much quicker than by car. And so, a quarter of an hour later, somewhat chilled, I was at the main gate of the prison.

The sergeant in charge of the checkpoint that afternoon was new and didn't know me. So he did everything according to the book. He examined my papers, took away my mobile phone, cross-checked my name. In the end he let me in, and I went through the usual series of steel doors which opened and closed as I passed, until I got to the lawyers' room. Which was the same as ever – as welcoming as the reception area of a provincial morgue.

They weren't in any hurry, and by the time my new client

arrived – at least a quarter of an hour later – I was thinking of setting fire to the table or a couple of chairs, to warm myself up and draw attention to myself.

I recognized him as soon as he came in, even though I hadn't seen him for more than twenty-five years.

Fabio Paolicelli, known as Fabio Rayban. We called him that because he always wore sunglasses, even at night. That was why I hadn't immediately recognized the name. For me, for everyone, he had always been Fabio Rayban.

It was the Seventies, which I remember as one long black-and-white TV news broadcast. The first images I have of that time are of the Piazza Fontana just after the bomb. I was seven years old, but I remember it all very well: the photos in the newspapers, the filmed reports on television, the conversations at home between my parents and friends who came to see them.

One afternoon – it may have been the day after the attack – I asked my grandpa Guido why they'd planted that bomb, if we were at war, and with what country. He looked at me and said nothing. It was the only time he couldn't answer one of my questions.

I remember almost all the important events of those years. I remember the faces of young men, the same age as us, gradually starting to appear on TV news broadcasts.

In those days I associated sporadically, without a great deal of conviction, with a number of far-left groups.

Fabio Rayban, on the other hand, was a Fascist thug.

Maybe more than just a thug. A lot of stories circulated about him, and others like him. Stories about armed robberies done for the sake of a daring gesture. About military camps in the remotest areas of the Murgia, attended by dubious characters from the armed forces and the secret services.

About so-called Aryan celebrations in luxurious villas on the outskirts of town. But the thing you heard most often about Rayban was that he had been part of the paramilitary squad that had stabbed to death an eighteen-year-old Communist who suffered from polio.

After a long trial, one of the Fascists was found guilty of the murder and then, very conveniently, killed himself in prison. Killing at the same time any possibility of identifying the others responsible.

In the days following the murder, Bari was filled with tear-gas smoke, the acrid smell of burnt cars, the sound of running footsteps on deserted pavements. Metal balls shattering windows. Sirens and blue flashing lights shattering the grey stillness of those late-November afternoons.

The Fascists were well organized. Just like criminals. They settled political arguments with iron rods, chains and knives. Sometimes guns, too. You just had to walk along the Via Sparano, in the vicinity of the church of San Ferdinando – an area considered a *black zone* – carrying the wrong newspaper or the wrong book, or even wearing the wrong clothes, and you ran the risk of beating beaten up.

And that's what happened to me.

I was fourteen and always wore a green anorak that I was very proud of. One afternoon I was strolling in the middle of town with two of my friends – the three of us little more than children – when we suddenly found ourselves surrounded. They were only sixteen, seventeen, but to us they were men. At that age two years' difference is a lifetime.

One of them was a tall, thin, fair-haired guy, with a face like David Bowie. He wore Ray-Bans, even though it was already dark. When he smiled, through thin lips, my blood ran cold.

A short, very sturdy-looking guy with a broken incisor approached me and told me I was a Red bastard and I should take off that fucking anorak immediately, or they might think of giving me what I deserved: the castor oil treatment.

In the mindless terror of that moment, I had no idea what he was talking about. Until then I'd never heard of the Fascist custom of pouring castor oil down their opponents' throats.

My friend Roberto peed himself. And I don't mean metaphorically. I saw the liquid stain spread over his discoloured jeans. In a thin voice, I asked why I had to take off my anorak. The short guy slapped me very hard between my cheek and my ear.

"Take it off, *comrade*."

I was terrified and felt like crying, but I didn't take off my anorak. Trying desperately to hold back my tears, I again asked why. The guy slapped me again, then punched me, then kicked me, then punched and slapped me some more. People passing by looked away.

I was on the ground, curled up to protect myself from the blows, when someone made them run away.

What happened next is clearer and more vivid in my memory.

A man helps me to my feet and asks me in a strong local accent if I want to go to casualty. I say no, I want to go home. I have my house keys, I add, as if he'd be interested, or as if it meant anything to him.

I walk away, and my friends aren't there any more, and I don't know when they disappeared. On the way home, I start crying. Not so much because of the pain I'm still feeling, but because of the humiliation and the fear. Few things leave such a strong impression as humiliation and fear.

Fucking Fascists.

And as I cry, and blow my nose, I say to myself out loud that despite everything I didn't take off my anorak. This thought makes me stiffen my spine and stop crying. I didn't take off my anorak, you fucking Fascists. And I remember your faces.

One day I'll get my own back on you.

*

When Paolicelli entered the lawyers' room, it all came back to me, in a rush. Like a sudden violent gust of wind that throws the windows wide open, causes the doors to slam, and scatters papers.

He held out his hand, and I hesitated for a moment before shaking it. I wondered if he noticed. Memories – vague things, noises, boys' voices, girls' voices, smells, cries of fear, songs by Inti-Illimani, the face of someone whose name I couldn't remember and who'd died of an overdose in the school toilets at the age of seventeen – crowded into my head like creatures suddenly released from a spell that has been keeping them prisoner in the basements or the attics of memory.

It was obvious he didn't remember me.

I waited a few moments, in order not to be too abrupt, before asking him why he had appointed me and why he was inside.

"They arrested me a year and a half ago for cross-border drug trafficking. I opted for the fast-track procedure in court and was given sixteen years, plus a fine so huge I can't even remember what it was."

You deserved it, you Fascist. You're paying the price now for all the things you did then.

"I was on my way back from a holiday in Montenegro. At the harbour in Bari the customs police were doing random checks on cars. They had dogs with them to sniff out drugs. When they got to my car the dogs seemed to go crazy. The customs police took me to their barracks and dismantled the car, and under the bodyshell they found forty kilos of high-quality cocaine."

Forty kilos of high-quality cocaine was certainly enough to justify the sentence he'd received, even with the fast-track procedure. But I didn't believe that the customs police had been doing random checks. Someone had tipped them off that a courier was bringing in a consignment, and they'd acted by the book in making it look as if the check was random. In order not to blow their informant's cover.

"The drugs weren't mine." Paolicelli's words broke into my thoughts.

"What do you mean, they weren't yours? Was there someone else in the car with you?"

"My wife and daughter were with me. We were on our way back from a week's holiday by the sea. And the drugs weren't mine. I don't know who put them there."

So that's it, I thought. He's ashamed that he was carrying the drugs in the same car where his wife and daughter were travelling. Typical of you Fascists: you're not even capable of being criminals with any dignity.

"I'm sorry, Paolicelli, but how could someone have planted those drugs without you knowing? I mean, we're talking about forty kilos, quite a lot to pack under the bodyshell of a car. I'm no expert on these things, but that must have taken time. Did you lend the car to anyone in Montenegro?"

"No, but for the whole of the holiday it was in the hotel car park. And the hotel porter had the keys; I had to leave them with him because the car park was full and sometimes a car had to be moved to make room. Someone, with the porter's knowledge, must have planted the drugs during the night, probably the night before we left. I assume they planned to retrieve them once we'd got through customs. Perhaps they had accomplices in Italy who'd do that for them. I know it sounds absurd, but the drugs weren't mine. I swear they weren't mine."

He was right. It did sound absurd.

You hear a lot of absurd stories like that in courtrooms, barracks, prisons. The commonest one is the one invariably told by people who've been found in possession of guns in full working order, with the hammer cocked. They all say they only just found the gun by chance, usually under a bush, or under a tree, or in a dustbin. They all say they've never handled a gun in their lives and that they were just on their way to hand it in to the police. That's why they were carrying it in their belt with the hammer cocked, somewhere near a jeweller's shop, for example, or the house of a gangland rival.

I felt like telling him that I didn't give a damn that he'd brought forty kilos of cocaine from Montenegro to Italy, and that I didn't give a damn if he had done it before, or how many times. So he might as well tell me the truth. It would make things a whole lot simpler. I was a criminal lawyer and it was my job to defend people like him. What would happen if I suddenly took it into my head to pass judgement on my clients? I felt like telling him these things, but I didn't. I suddenly realized what was happening in my head, and I didn't like it.

I realized that I wanted him to confess. I wanted to be absolutely certain that he was guilty, so that I could help him to get the long gaol sentence he deserved, without any problems of conscience or professional ethics.

I realized that I wanted to be his judge – and maybe also his executioner – rather than his lawyer. I had an old score to settle.

And that wasn't right. I told myself I ought to think about it, because if I didn't think I could control that urge, then I ought to give up on the idea of defending him. Or rather, I shouldn't agree to it in the first place.

"What happened after you were arrested?"

"After they found the drugs, they tried to get me to cooperate with them. They told me they wanted to do a . . . what's it called?"

"A controlled delivery?"

"That's it, a controlled delivery. They told me they'd let me drive the car away with the drugs still in it. I would deliver the drugs as if nothing had happened. They would follow me and when the moment was right they would arrest the people who were waiting for the consignment. They told me I would get a greatly reduced sentence, maybe as little as three years. I told them I had no idea where to take the drugs because they weren't mine. So then they said they were arresting me and they were also arresting my wife because it was obvious we were in cahoots. I started to panic and I told them, yes, the drugs were mine, but she didn't know anything. They phoned the prosecutor and he told them to take my statement and arrest me, but only me. So they took down my confession, arrested me and let my wife go."

He was speaking calmly, but with an undercurrent of desperation.

He asked me for a cigarette and I told him I didn't have any because I'd quit a couple of years ago. He hadn't smoked for ten years either, he said. He'd started again the day after he went into prison.

Who had he appointed as his defence counsel when he was arrested? And why had he decided to change now? From the way he looked at me before replying, it was clear he'd been expecting the question.

"When they arrested me, they asked me who my lawyer was, so that they could inform him. I didn't have a lawyer and I told them I didn't know who to appoint. My wife was still there – a friend had come to collect our daughter – and I told her to get advice from someone about finding a good lawyer. The next day she appointed someone."

"And who did she appoint?"

This was where the really strange part of the affair started, if Paolicelli was telling the truth.

"My wife was just leaving home when she was approached by a man who said he was acting on behalf of some friends who wanted to help us. He told her to appoint a lawyer from Rome named Corrado Macrì, who would sort things out for me. He gave her a piece of paper with this lawyer's name and a mobile number and told her to appoint him straight away, so that he could visit me in prison before I was interrogated by the examining magistrate."

"And what did your wife do?"

Paolicelli's wife, who was at her wits' end and didn't know any lawyers, appointed this Macrì. A few hours later, he arrived from Rome, as if he'd been waiting to be appointed by her and didn't have any other work at the moment. He visited Paolicelli in prison and told him not to worry, he'd sort it all out. When Paolicelli asked him who had engaged him and who the man was who had approached his wife, he again told him not to worry; as long as he heeded his,

Macrì's, advice, everything would be fine. His first piece of advice was to exercise his right to remain silent at that first interview with the examining magistrate or he might make the situation worse.

I wondered by what stretch of the imagination the situation could have been made *worse*, but I didn't say that to Paolicelli.

They appealed the arrest, but the custody order was confirmed.

I didn't see how there could have been any other decision. But I didn't say that either.

Macrì then appealed against the decision on the grounds that there had been a procedural irregularity – he didn't specify what it was – which gave him high hopes that he could have the proceedings declared invalid.

His high hopes turned out to be unfounded because the custody order was confirmed again. But that didn't dent Macrì's optimism. He told Paolicelli and his wife not to worry, to be patient, and he would sort everything out. According to Paolicelli, he said this in a knowing tone, like someone who has the right cards up his sleeve and will play them when the time is right.

When they got to the preliminary hearing, Macrì again advised Paolicelli not to say anything, and they opted for the fast-track procedure. The result of that, I already knew.

"And what did Macrì say then?"

"Again he told me not to worry, he would sort everything out."

"Was he joking?"

"No. He said he wasn't surprised at the result – after weeks of telling me that at worst I'd only get four or five years – and that the appeal court would be sure to reduce the sentence.

It was when I read the appeal he prepared – a one-page document with almost nothing written on it – that I blew my top."

"What happened?"

"I told him he was gambling with my life. I told him I knew perfectly well who had sent him. And then I told him I was pissed off and that I'd call the examining magistrate and tell him everything."

"What was it you were going to tell the magistrate?"

"There wasn't anything specific. I only said it in the heat of anger, to shake him up a bit. The fact is, I have no idea who sent him. But he must have believed me, he must have thought I really did have something important to tell."

"And what did he say?"

"He turned really nasty. He told me I should be very careful about what I did, and especially about what I said. He said accidents sometimes happen in prison to people who can't keep their mouths shut."

I noticed that he was panting a little. He had to take a breath before starting again.

"I didn't have anything to tell the magistrate. Apart from the fact that the drugs weren't mine. He wouldn't have believed me. You haven't."

I was about to reply. Then I told myself that he was right. So I said nothing and let him continue.

"Anyway, he told me that if I didn't trust him any more there was no reason for him to continue as my lawyer. He was dropping the case, but I should remember what he'd said. If I asked to speak to a magistrate, *they* would know immediately. Then he left."

Now I was the one who needed a cigarette. It didn't happen often – usually only when things were getting complicated.

And if Paolicelli was telling the truth, this whole business was complicated, to say the least.

"Oh, I nearly forgot something."

"What?"

"He didn't ask me for money. Despite all the times he came to Bari, all the expenses he must have incurred, he didn't want to be paid. I said I wanted to pay him something and he told me not to worry, that when we had sorted everything out – he always talked about *sorting everything out* – I could buy him a present. Then, when he got the prosecutor to lift the sequestration order on the car, which is in my wife's name, he offered to collect it personally. I don't think that's normal conduct for a lawyer."

No, it wasn't normal conduct for a lawyer at all.

This whole business of the lawyer was strange. Too convoluted to have been made up. I didn't know what I was dealing with. I was thinking hard, and he must have realized that, because he didn't interrupt me. Was it possible that the drugs really weren't his? Could someone really have thought up this method of transporting large quantities of cocaine? The more I thought about it, the more schizophrenic my reflections became. On the one hand, I told myself this was just meaningless speculation, things like that only happened in films or novels. On the other hand, the idea that Paolicelli could be telling the truth seemed both appalling and very plausible. The whole affair was like one of those magic cards I used to find in the packets of processed cheese when I was a child: depending on how you moved them the image changed, the figure moved, and other figures appeared. This case was like a magic card, with murky figures and a vague feeling of rottenness as soon as you go too close to it.

I told him this was enough for the moment. I had to look at

the papers, to get a better idea of the case. He said his wife had a copy of the whole file and she would bring it to my office before the end of the week.

He asked me how much he should pay me as an advance and I replied that I had to look at the papers before I could agree to take on the case, especially as a colleague was involved. He nodded and didn't ask me any more questions.

I had already stood up and was recovering my raincoat when I thought of something I needed to know before I left.

"Why me? I mean, why did you choose me?"

He gave me a strange smile. He'd been expecting the question. "People talk a lot in prison. They talk a lot about judges, and about prosecutors. Which ones are good, which ones are stupid, which ones are clever, or dangerous, or corrupt. And they talk about defence lawyers."

He broke off and looked at me. He could tell from my face that he had me hooked.

"Which ones are efficient but stupid. Which ones are honest but incompetent and never stand up to the judges. Which ones are arse lickers. Which ones can cut corners – or claim that they can – to get what they want. They say a lot of things about defence lawyers."

Another pause, another look. My face hadn't changed. He was searching for the right words.

"What they say about you is that you aren't afraid."

"In what way?"

"They say that if you believe in something, you don't give up. They say you're a good person."

I felt a slight tingling in my scalp and down my back.

"And they say you're very good at your job."

I didn't know what to say.

"Get me out of here," he went on, and his voice cracked, as if he no longer had the strength to control himself. "I'm innocent, I swear it. I have a daughter. She's the only thing that matters in my life. I haven't seen her since I was arrested. I didn't want her to visit me in prison, so I haven't seen her since that damned morning."

The last words were halfway been a gasp and a whisper.

I had to go. I had to get out of there. I told him I would study the papers as soon as I got them, and then we would meet again and talk about them. We shook hands and I left.

3

I didn't even have to look at the papers, I told myself that evening, at home.

I couldn't defend Fabio Rayban. All the things that had gone through my head when I'd recognized him should have set alarm bells ringing. I couldn't ignore them.

I had to act maturely and professionally.

Paolicelli was probably guilty and had been given the right sentence. But that was why he had a right to be defended professionally, by someone who didn't have my inner reservations and didn't have an old score to settle with him.

I had to turn down the case without even reading the papers. It would be better for everyone.

It would be *right*.

In a few days' time, I'd go back to the prison and tell him I couldn't defend him. I would either tell him the truth, or invent an excuse.

But one thing was certain. I couldn't take the case.

4

Maria Teresa knocked at my door, put her head round it, and told me Signora Kawabata was here.

"Who?"

She came in, closed the door, and said that Signora Kawabata had come about the Paolicelli case.

"But Kawabata is a Japanese name."

"I guess so. She looks Japanese, anyway."

"And what has she got to do with Paolicelli?"

"Quite a lot, she's his wife. She says she has copies of the documents."

When she came in, I recognized her immediately.

She said good afternoon, shook hands with me, and sat down in front of the desk without taking off her coat or even undoing it. I could smell perfume, essence of amber, with a hint of something more pungent that I couldn't quite identify. Close up, she looked a bit older and even more beautiful than she had a few days before in the courtroom.

"I'm Fabio Paolicelli's wife. I've brought you all the papers relating to the trial and the sentence."

Bizarrely, she had a slight Neapolitan accent. She emptied her bag, placed a bundle of photocopies on the desk and asked me if we could talk for a few minutes. Of course we could talk. That's what I'm paid for, after all.

"I need to know if there's any hope for Fabio's appeal, and if so how much."

She'd come straight to the point. The right thing to do, from her point of view. But I couldn't come straight to the point, and not only because I wanted to sound professional.

"It's impossible to say right now. I have to read all the papers on the case, including the original ruling."

And I also have to decide if I'm going to take on the case. But I didn't say that.

"Fabio told you what this is all about."

I was getting impatient. Did she expect me to form an opinion on the basis of what the defendant had told me in prison?

"He told me the gist of it, but as I was saying . . ."

"I don't suppose there's much hope of an acquittal, even on appeal. But I've been told it may be possible to plea-bargain. Fabio could get as little as six or seven years. In three or four years he could be allowed home visits . . . or perhaps . . . what is it called?"

"It's called day release."

I found her tone a bit irritating. I don't generally like clients – or worse still, the relatives of clients – who've swotted up on the law and tell you what you can and can't do.

"You see, signora" – I hated the self-important tone in my own voice as soon as I opened my mouth – "as I was saying, I have to study all the papers before I can express a sound opinion. To think of alternatives, including plea-bargaining, I really need to have a clearer idea of the case. There may be procedural or technical questions that a lay person might be unaware of."

In other words, I'm the lawyer here. You stick to flower arranging, or the tea ceremony, or whatever. And I haven't even decided yet if I'm going to defend your husband – who's a Fascist thug and probably also a drug trafficker – because

I've had a score to settle with him and his friends for thirty years.

Those were the very words I had in my mind. I didn't even realize that I'd moved quickly from being sure I'd refuse the case to being undecided about whether or not I'd accept it.

She grimaced, which only made her look even more beautiful.

It had been a lawyer's answer, and she didn't like it. She wanted me to calm her fears in some way. Even if it meant telling her there was no alternative to plea-bargaining. People want many things from a lawyer, but what they want more than anything is for him to take away the anguish of having to deal with policemen, prosecutors, judges and court proceedings. With all the apparatus of what's called justice. They want the lawyer to take away the anguish of thinking.

"Going on what your husband told me, this isn't an easy case. If things happened in the exact terms" – exact terms? Why the hell was I talking this way? – "in which he told them to me, then this isn't going to be an easy appeal. In fact, it's going to be very hard, which means that plea-bargaining is definitely a possibility we'd have to consider seriously. On the other hand . . ."

"On the other hand?"

"Your husband says he's innocent. Obviously, if he's innocent, the idea of plea-bargaining and ending up with seven or eight years, even supposing we could get it down as much as that, is a bit hard to take. Even if there is the prospect of home visits and day release."

She hadn't been expecting that answer. She realized that she had kept her coat on and she unbuttoned it nervously, as if she suddenly felt hot or stifled. I asked her if she wanted to take it off and give it to me to hang up. She said no, thanks. But then she took it off and placed it over her legs.

"Do you really think he might be innocent?"

There. I'd asked for it.

"Look, Signora Paolicelli, I really can't answer that question. In most cases we lawyers don't know the truth. We don't know if our client is guilty or innocent. In many ways it's better not to know, it's easier to defend the client in a professional way . . ."

"You don't believe his story, do you?"

I took a deep breath, resisting the impulse to talk more bullshit. "I'll be able to get a clearer idea after I've read the papers. But I must admit, your husband's story is very hard to believe."

"I don't know if his story is true either. I don't know if he's been telling me the truth, even though he swears that the drugs weren't his. He's sworn it to me over and over. Sometimes I believe him, and sometimes I think he's denying everything because he's ashamed and doesn't want to admit he was carrying drugs in the same car as me and our daughter."

That's what I think too. It's the likeliest hypothesis, and it's probably true.

I told myself these things as I looked at her in silence, my face devoid of expression. And as I looked at her I realized something.

It wasn't true that she had doubts about her husband's innocence. She was *convinced* her husband was guilty, and that, more than anything else, had been her curse since the whole affair had started.

"Fabio told me you'd have to read the file first before you decided whether or not to accept the case. Do you mind if

27

I ask why? Does it mean that if you're convinced he's guilty you won't defend him?"

That was a question I really needed. No, I don't give a damn whether he's guilty or not. I defend guilty people every day. It's just that your husband – I don't know if he ever told you this – has a past as a criminal and maybe a murderer, or at least an accomplice to murder. I say this from personal knowledge, I hope I'm making myself clear. Given all this, I don't know if I'm capable of defending him properly.

I didn't say that.

I told her that this was the way I worked. I had to examine the papers first. I didn't like to take on a case sight unseen. It was a lie, but one I couldn't help telling.

"When will you let me know if you accept?"

"It isn't a very big file. I could look at it over the weekend and give you my answer on Monday, or Tuesday at the latest."

She took a large man's-style wallet out of her handbag. "Fabio told me you didn't want an advance before deciding whether to accept or not. But you're going to read the file, and that's work, so . . ."

I raised my open hands and shook my head. I didn't want any money for the moment. Thanks all the same, but this was the way I worked. She didn't insist. Instead of taking money or a cheque from the wallet she took a business card and handed it to me.

Natsu Kawabata, Japanese Cuisine, it said. Beneath that, two telephone numbers, one home and one mobile. I looked up from the card, questioningly.

She told me she was a chef. Three evenings a week she worked in a restaurant – she mentioned the name of a fashionable spot – but she also made sushi, sashimi and tempura for private parties thrown by people who could afford it. Japanese food has never come cheap.

The words escaped me before I could stop them. "I'd have said you were a model or something like that, not a chef." I regretted saying it before I'd even finished the sentence. I felt like a complete idiot.

But she smiled. It was only the hint of a smile, but it was very beautiful.

"I used to be a model." The smile disappeared. "That was how I met Fabio, in Milan. It seems like a long time ago, so many things have changed."

She left the sentence hanging in the air, and in the brief silence that followed I tried to imagine how their relationship had begun, why they'd moved from Milan to Bari. Other things, too.

She was the one who broke the silence and interrupted my thoughts. "But I like cooking more. Are you familiar with Japanese cuisine?"

I said yes, I was very familiar with it and liked it a lot.

In that case, she said, I ought to try her version of it some time.

It was the kind of thing you say to be polite, I thought.

But a shiver went through me, the kind you feel when you're sixteen and the prettiest girl in the class suddenly, amazingly, stops and talks to you in the school corridor.

Natsu asked me to call her as soon as I'd read the papers and had decided what to do.

She left, and it occurred to me that she hadn't said a word about having come to court and watched me at work. I wondered why, and couldn't find an answer.

A slight scent of amber lingered in the air. With that hint of something more pungent that I couldn't quite identify.

5

A few minutes before nine, Maria Teresa came in and asked me if I still needed anything, as she was about to leave. I asked her to order me a pizza and a beer before she left. She looked at me with an expression that said it's Friday evening, do you think it's right to stay in the office eating a disgusting pizza, drinking a disgusting beer and working?

I looked back at her, with an expression that said yes, I do think it's right, especially as I don't have anything better to do. Anyway I don't want to do anything better.

To be honest, I don't even want to think about it.

She looked as if she was about to say something, but thought better of it. She would order the pizza, she said, and she'd see me on Monday morning.

I ate the pizza, drank the beer, cleared up the desk, put the latest Leonard Cohen album, *Dear Heather*, on the CD player and settled down to look through the papers Signora Natsu Kawabata had brought in.

Kawabata – like the writer, I thought. What was the title of that story? *House of the Sleeping Beauties*, wasn't it? Yasunari Kawabata. A lovely, sad story. I ought to reread it, I thought. Maybe Natsu was related to the Kawabata who'd won the Nobel Prize. She could even be his granddaughter.

What a brilliant thought, I told myself. Absolutely brilliant. Like a Japanese person meeting a Signor Rossi and thinking, "Ah, his name's Rossi, I wonder if he's related to the motorcyclist."

I think it's best if I read the file.

It didn't take long. The story was pretty much the way Paolicelli had told it. The arrest and custody records mentioned a routine check by the customs police in the harbour area, using dogs trained to sniff out drugs. I thought the same thing I'd thought the day before, when Paolicelli had told me his story. The customs police had probably had a tip-off. On the blank sheet of paper I'd placed next to the file I jotted down: *Why the check?* Then I told myself it was a question that was likely to remain unanswered, and I went on.

With the records were Paolicelli's statements.

They were headed *Transcript of statements made by the accused of his own free will.* Of his own free will, of course. The transcript was very short and, after a few preliminaries, the gist of it was in this sentence:

"I acknowledge that the quantity of forty kilos of cocaine was discovered in my car. Regarding this, I freely declare that the drugs belong to myself alone and that my wife Natsu Kawabata, whose full particulars have been noted in other documents, has no connection whatsoever with this illegal transportation, which is the sole responsibility of the undersigned. I placed the narcotics in the car without my wife's knowledge. I have no intention of naming the persons from whom I acquired the aforementioned quantity of narcotics, nor those to whom I was supposed to deliver them. I have nothing to add."

Read, confirmed and signed.

On my sheet of notes, I jotted down: *Usability of statements?*

That meant that there were serious doubts about the

validity and usability of these statements, which had been made without a lawyer being present. It wasn't much to go on, but considering the situation I couldn't afford to overlook anything.

I went quickly on to the report of the customs police, which mostly reiterated what was in the arrest and custody records. Then the transcript of Paolicelli's interrogation by the examining magistrate, in which my putative client stated that he was exercising his right to remain silent. It was here that Avvocato Corrado Macrì made his first appearance.

On the sheet of notes I wrote: *Avvocato Macrì, who the fuck are you?*

The nice thing about these personal notes is that you can write whatever you like, including obscenities. As far as I'm concerned, swear words help me to think. If I can write a few nice expletives in my notes, my ideas seem to flow more easily.

Sometimes, though, I leave these notes where I shouldn't. Among the documents to be attached to an appeal, for example, or a lodging of a civil action.

Usually Maria Teresa checks everything, discovers these entertaining screeds, gets rid of them, and saves my reputation. Usually.

Once when she was off ill, I was forced to be my own secretary for a couple of days. One of the things I did during those two days was to file a motion for a client of mine to be placed under house arrest. This client had set up a number of paper companies and conjured away several million euros.

The Prosecutor's Department and the customs police had started taking an interest in him, had discovered his fraud, and had thrown him in prison. A lawyer shouldn't say such things, but they'd done their job well.

My motion referred to some documents which proved that my client – Signor Saponaro, an accountant and a well-known homosexual – was not quite as guilty as had at first appeared. It pointed out the amount of time my client had already spent in prison – three months – and asked for the custody order against him to be mitigated, since it was "not indispensable for measures as harsh as imprisonment to be applied". The usual litany.

A few days after I had filed the motion I had a call from the clerk of the court. The judge wanted to speak to me? I'd be right there, of course, but could I possibly know what it was all about? So that I could be prepared. Oh, he hadn't said what he wanted to see me about. All right, just give me time to leave my office and get to the courthouse.

Half an hour later I was in the judge's office.

"Good morning, Consigliere. You sent for me." I smiled, and gave him a politely questioning look.

"Good morning, Avvocato. Yes, I sent for you because I wanted to show you this." He took a small sheet of paper from a red folder. "I think this is yours. Should I consider it an attachment to your motion on behalf of Signor Saponaro?"

He handed me the sheet of paper. They were the notes I had made while writing the motion. I felt a distant rumbling in my head, like a huge wave or a herd of buffalo coming closer. I went red.

The gist of what I had written revolved around the not very legal concept of "raging queen, and a thief to boot". Anyone giving that screed even a cursory glance would have been in no doubt that the "raging queen, and a thief to boot" was Signor Saponaro and that his lawyer – who was me – wasn't privately convinced that his client was innocent.

I tried to find something to say to the judge, to try and excuse this disaster. Of course I couldn't find anything.

So I asked him if, for the purpose of my forthcoming disbarment, he intended to report me personally or if he preferred me to report myself. I hastened to add that it didn't really make much difference. I did, however, beg him not to advertise the unfortunate expression I had used – "raging queen" – a cryptic allusion to my client's sexual tastes. It was a stupid lapse, which, if known, would have done irreparable damage to my reputation, not only as a lawyer, but as a man of the left.

The judge had a sense of humour. He gave me back the sheet of paper and didn't report me.

He didn't accept my motion on behalf of Signor Saponaro either, but that really would have been too much to ask for.

*

There was not much else in the file that was of any significance.

There was a toxicologist's report on the narcotics. The cocaine was 68 per cent pure, in other words, of high quality. It was possible, the expert wrote, to extract hundreds of thousands of doses from it for reselling.

There were Paolicelli's mobile phone records, and his wife's. The customs police had acquired them to see if they could identify any interesting contacts, immediately before or immediately after the car had been stopped and searched and the drugs found. Clearly they had found nothing of interest, because the records had been sent to the prosecutor's department accompanied only by a brief note saying: *No significant contact has emerged from the telephone records.*

There was the order for Paolicelli to be remanded in custody, no more than ten lines, and there was the sentence. Even that, to tell the truth, wasn't very long. But what else was there to write? "The guilt of the defendant has been satisfactorily proved to the required standard of evidence. He was carrying the narcotics on board his car and, moreover, freely admitted his responsibility before being arrested. On this basis it would seem literally impossible to suggest any plausible alternative hypothesis, and indeed no such hypothesis was put forward, even by the defendant himself, who, when interrogated by the examining magistrate, exercised – understandably in view of the weakness of his position – his right to remain silent."

With my pen I circled the words *plausible alternative hypothesis*. That was the problem. That's always the problem in criminal trials. Supplying a *plausible* alternative explanation for the evidence presented by the prosecution.

What alternative hypothesis could possibly be put forward in a case like this?

The only one was that Paolicelli had told me the truth and that someone else – God knows how, God knows when – had put the drugs in the car. But if his story was true, then Paolicelli was in deep, deep shit.

Could someone really have wanted to set Paolicelli up by planting the drugs in his car and then tipping off the customs police?

I immediately ruled this out. You don't throw away forty kilos of cocaine just to set someone up. If you want to set someone up, you plant ten grams on him, divided into forty doses, then there's no doubt he's intending to sell the stuff, and you've achieved your aim. Efficiently and cheaply.

No, they couldn't possibly have planted forty kilos on him

just to get him arrested. Someone may well have tipped off the customs police that a consignment of top-quality cocaine was coming in from Montenegro in that car. But whoever it was couldn't have been the owner of the drugs, or anyone else who'd planted them just to ruin Signor Fabio Rayban.

So let's rule out the theory that whoever planted the drugs in the car was the same person who tipped off the customs police. And let's assume that Paolicelli is telling the truth. If he really is innocent, how the hell to prove it?

Find out who planted the drugs, I told myself.

Well, that should be easy enough. All I have to do is uncover the network of international traffickers who planted the drugs, drag them to the appeal court to testify, and there, stricken by remorse, they confess, thus clearing my client. He's acquitted, justice triumphs, and the legend of Avvocato Guerrieri is secure.

If Paolicelli really was innocent, then this was the worst case that had come my way in the whole of my so-called career, I told myself as I leafed through the last pages. At the bottom of the file I found a copy of Paolicelli's criminal record. It was pretty much as I'd expected. Some very old convictions as a minor for affray, actual bodily harm, possession of weapons. All of them during the years when the Fascist gangs were active. Nothing since 1981.

As I looked through the record, I caught myself thinking that, until a few hours earlier, I'd been determined *not* to take the case.

Until Signora Natsu Kawabata had stepped into my office.

6

I put my notes in order. More than that, I tried to get my ideas in order.

For Paolicelli to have a chance of getting out of this – which was very unlikely – I would have to do a bit of investigating, and that was where the problems started.

I'd only ever used private detectives a couple of times, with disastrous results. And that was in cases which were – how shall I put it? – a lot less problematic than the Paolicelli case. After the second time, I had sworn it would also be the last.

I realized I'd have to talk to Carmelo Tancredi.

Carmelo Tancredi is a police inspector who specializes in hunting down the worst dregs of humanity: rapists, sexual abusers, child traffickers.

He has the mild, slightly downtrodden appearance of a Mexican peasant in a B-western, the kind of intuition you usually only find in fictional policemen, and the grip of a crazed pitbull.

I'd talk to him and ask him what he thought of this whole business. If it was really possible that someone had planted the drugs in Paolicelli's car in Montenegro with the intention of retrieving them in Italy. And I would ask him if he thought it was worth conducting an investigation to try and clear my client.

Then I would ask around to see if anyone knew this lawyer, Macrì. To find out where he fitted into the jigsaw.

Assuming, of course, that there was a jigsaw. There could be a much simpler explanation: the drugs did in fact belong to Paolicelli and some unknown accomplices, the lawyer – as often happens in these cases – had been hired and paid by these accomplices, and his wife, of course, knew nothing about it.

The fact that I now had a plan – talking to Tancredi, inquiring about this Macrì – gave me the feeling that I'd actually got somewhere. I looked at my watch and realized it was two in the morning.

For a moment, only for a moment, I remembered Margherita's face. Before it dissolved into the photographic negative of that September afternoon, and then disappeared in the distance, somewhere to the west.

Great Friday night, I thought as I left the office and headed home.

7

On Monday morning, I asked Maria Teresa to call Signora Kawabata and tell her that I was taking the case and that I would visit her husband in prison before the end of the week. She – Maria Teresa – would have to go to the clerk of the court's office at the court of appeal to check if a date had been fixed for the hearing.

At that point I hesitated, as if there was something else, something I'd forgotten. Maria Teresa asked me if she should tell Signora Kawabata to come to the office to pay an advance and I said yes, that was it, that was what I had forgotten. She had to tell her to come to the office. To pay an advance.

Of course.

Then I took the papers I needed for that morning's hearings and left.

Outside, it was freezing cold and I told myself I didn't have to take the bicycle every time, I could actually walk. I went into the bar on the ground floor of the building where my office was, had a cappuccino, and on the way to the courtroom called Carmelo Tancredi.

"Guido! Don't tell me one of those maggots we arrested last night is a client of yours. Please don't tell me that."

"OK, I won't. Who did you arrest last night?"

"A paedophile ring organizing holidays in Thailand. Vermin for export. We've been working on the case for six months.

Two of our undercover officers infiltrated the ring, even went on holiday with these animals, and collected evidence by the barrel load. Incredibly, the Thai police cooperated."

"And you arrested them last night?"

"Right. You can't imagine the kind of stuff we found in their homes."

"I can't imagine and I don't want to know."

That was only half true. I didn't want to know, but I could imagine only too well what they might have found when they searched the men's homes. I'd occasionally been involved in paedophilia cases – always representing the victims – and had seen the kind of material taken from people like that. In comparison, photographs of autopsies are quite pleasant to look at.

"Since, fortunately, you're not the lawyer of one of these maggots, why are you calling me?"

"I wanted to buy you a coffee and have a little chat. But if you worked all night and are just now going to sleep, it doesn't matter. I realize you're getting on in years, so . . ."

He said something in broad Sicilian. I didn't really understand the words but I could guess that he was making a gently critical comment on my sense of humour.

Then he went back to Italian. He told me I had to wait until they'd taken statements from the people they'd arrested and done all the other paperwork. He said he'd have to check it all because the guys in his squad were very good when it came to working in the field – tailing suspects, stakeouts, knocking down doors, chasing people, grabbing them, maybe even manhandling them a little, which doesn't come amiss sometimes – but you had to keep them under strict supervision whenever they got their hands on a computer, or had to deal with legal formalities. He would be finished around midday and so, if I wanted, I could come by and pick him up at police headquarters and buy him an aperitif.

OK, I said, I'd pick him up at twelve-thirty.

Then I went to the courthouse and pleaded my various cases. At my usual pace, in a kind of semi-conscious state.

During my first years in the profession – as a trainee and then when I was already a prosecutor – what I'd liked best was arriving at the courthouse in the morning. I'd arrive twenty minutes before the start of the hearings, say hello to a few friends, go and have a coffee, smoke a cigarette – in those days they let you smoke in the corridors. Sometimes I might also meet a girl I liked and make plans for the evening.

Little by little these rituals had become more sporadic and then disappeared. It was something physiological, the kind of thing that happens inevitably once you pass thirty. Over time, I'd gradually fallen out of love with that moment of entering the courthouse, the ritual coffee and all the rest of it. Sometimes I would look around, on the way to the bar. I would look at the young lawyers, often well-dressed, even too well-dressed. I would look at the girls – secretaries, trainees, even a few young magistrates on probation.

They all seemed a little stupid to me, and I'd think, tritely, that when *we* were young we were different, and better.

Not a very clever thought, but once you get started on something like that you can't stop. If these people are so dumb, then there's no reason to envy them, no reason to envy their youth, their supple joints, their infinite possibilities. They're idiots, you can see that from the way they behave, at the bar, and everywhere. We were better, and we still are, so why envy them?

Why, damn it?

By twelve-twenty I was outside police headquarters. I called

Tancredi to tell him to come down and join me. When I saw him, I thought he looked like someone who's slept on a sofa, with his coat and shoes on. For all I knew, he probably had.

We hadn't seen each other for a while, so the first thing he did was to ask after Margherita. I told him she'd been away for a few months on business, and tried to look as natural and as neutral as possible as I told him this. I could tell from his expression that I didn't quite manage it. So I changed the subject and asked him about his thesis. Tancredi had already done all his psychology exams, and only needed to finish his thesis to graduate. He said he hadn't been working on it for a while, and from the way he said it I realized I'd touched on a sore point, too.

We were quits. We could go and have our aperitif now.

We chose a wine bar a few hundred yards from police headquarters, run by a friend of Tancredi's. It was a place that tended to be busiest at night. Right now, it was deserted, and an ideal place for a quiet chat.

We ordered oysters and a white Sicilian wine. We ate a first tray of oysters and both agreed we hadn't had enough. So we ordered more, and drank several glasses of wine.

After his last oyster, Tancredi put his cigar stub in his mouth – he almost always had one with him, and almost never lit it – moved his chair back and asked me what I wanted from him. I told him the whole Paolicelli story, trying not to leave out any detail. When I'd finished, I said I needed his advice.

With the hand that was holding the cigar stub, he signalled to me to go on.

"First of all, have you ever heard of drugs being transported to Italy by being planted in cars belonging to people who didn't know anything about them? Have there ever been any cases in which something like that has cropped up?"

"Oh yes, it's cropped up. Turkish heroin traffickers used to use a system like that. They'd target Italian tourists who'd driven to Turkey by car. They'd steal the car, fill it with heroin and then make sure it was recovered before anyone went to the police to report it. And the person who recovered it even got a reward for his good deed. Then the tourists would set off back to Italy, and the Turks would follow them at a distance, to make sure nothing happened to the consignment. If the car was stopped and searched at the border, the problem was entirely the unsuspecting tourist's. Once across the border, their Italian friends would come into the picture. At the first opportunity the car would be stolen again, the only difference being that this time it wasn't given back. End of story."

"How far back are we talking?"

"As far as I know, this modus operandi has definitely been established on two separate occasions. Once in a big investigation by the Prosecutor's Department and Flying Squad in Trieste, and once in Bari by our own Drugs Squad. This was three, four years ago."

I rubbed my face, against the direction of the stubble. So, theoretically, Paolicelli could have been telling the truth, even though he hadn't said anything about the car being stolen. The story of the hotel porter made sense.

"And do you know about operations of this kind where the car hasn't been stolen?"

"What do you mean? They plant the drugs and just leave them there as a gift?"

"Very funny. I meant, where they don't steal the car to plant the drugs in the first place."

As he replied, I got the distinct impression he wasn't telling me everything he knew.

"I don't know of anything like that, but it isn't impossible. If you know where the car is and you have the time, you don't have to steal it, you can take it and bring it back without the owner even realizing."

"For the sake of argument: if you were a private detective and you were given the job of clearing Paolicelli's name, what would you do?"

"For the sake of argument, right? First of all, I'm not a private detective. Secondly, I don't think we've established that your new client is innocent. It's *possible* someone's car could be full of drugs that aren't his, I grant you. But the fact that it's possible doesn't mean it happened in this case. The most realistic hypothesis —"

"I hate logical policemen. I know, the most realistic hypothesis is that the drugs were his. If someone has a car full of cocaine, the first thing you consider is that the cocaine was his. Having said that, if you were a private detective . . ."

"If I were a private detective, before I said a word or moved a finger, I'd make sure I got a big advance. Then the first thing I'd do would be to question our friend Paolicelli again. His wife, too. Who, I suspect, isn't at all bad-looking."

Tancredi was capable of reading a lot of things in a person's face. Right then, I wished he wasn't.

"I'd try to find out if there really is a reason to suspect the hotel porter. Though I don't know how far we'd get."

"What do you mean?"

"To find out anything definite about the porter, or any of the hotel staff, there'd have to be an official investigation. We'd have to ask the police in Montenegro for cooperation. I don't know if you remember who we're talking about. For years, some of the police chiefs over there, and a few of their ministers, ran the international trade in contraband cigarettes."

I did remember.

"Anyway, I'd ask Paolicelli and his wife if they noticed anything strange during the holiday, especially towards the end. Even insignificant details. If they met anyone, a person who was very pleasant, tried to make friends with them. If they chatted to anyone, and this person asked a lot of questions. Where are you from, when did you arrive, and especially, when are you going home? And I'd ask them to tell me everything they remember about the porter, or the owners of the hotel, or anyone on the staff – a waiter for example – who caught their attention for any reason."

"And then?"

"It depends on what they answer. If it does turns out that there was someone snooping on them in Montenegro, you'd need to check if by any chance this person also travelled back on the same ferry."

"And how can I check that?"

He pretended to look downhearted. "That's just it. You can't."

"Come on, Carmelo, please help me. I just want to know if he told me a pack of lies or if he's really innocent. If he is, that's really tough on him."

He didn't reply immediately. He rolled the cigar stub between his index finger and thumb, looking at it as if it were an object of great interest, ignoring me for a few seconds, as if he was wondering what to tell me. In the end, he shrugged.

"It's possible your client is telling the truth. A few months ago an informant of mine told me there were some major consignments of cocaine coming in from Albania, Montenegro and Croatia, using precisely that method. Planting the drugs in a car without even stealing it."

"Shit."

"They fill the car, a day or two before their unwitting courier leaves. Then one of the gang gets on the ferry to keep an eye on the merchandise. Once past customs, they get to the final phase: at the first opportunity, their accomplices in Italy steal the car and recover the drugs."

"Is there an ongoing investigation into all this?"

"No, at least not as far as I know. I passed the information on to the drugs squad. The only thing they said was that they'd like to know who my informant was so they could talk to him."

He made a disgusted face. A real cop never asks a colleague to tell him the name of his informant. Only amateurs or rogues do that.

"And you told them to fuck off."

"But very politely."

"So the information was never used."

"As far as I know. In any case that's not what interests us. You need to talk to your client and his lovely wife and get anything from them that they can remember. Then, depending on what they tell you, we may be able to find some way of checking it out."

"OK, Carmelo, I'll talk to them and get them to tell me everything. But then you have to help me. For instance, we could get hold of the passenger list from the ferry. To see if there's any name on it that matches your records. You won't have to do much, just talk to some of your colleagues in the border police and —"

"Do you want me to wash your car windows, too? Just to make sure you get the full service."

"As a matter of fact, it's been a while since —"

Again, Tancredi said something in broad Sicilian. It sounded pretty similar to what he had said a few hours earlier on the phone.

In the end, though, he told me to call him after I'd talked to Paolicelli.

"If anything useful comes out of your chat, we'll see if we can take it any further. Another thing you could do in the meantime is try and find out some more about that colleague of yours who turned up from Rome. If Paolicelli and his wife are telling the truth, this guy has a connection with the owners of the drugs. Knowing who this lawyer is could give us a lead."

Right. Our little chat had borne fruit. I felt quite pleased.

I stood up and went to the cash desk to pay the bill, but the owner told me that no one was allowed to pay without Tancredi's permission.

And I didn't have his permission that day.

8

Natsu Kawabata came to the office on Tuesday afternoon.

She was wearing the same blue coat as the last time. She looked more beautiful every time I saw her.

It was obvious she was of mixed Japanese and European blood. As her name was Kawabata, I assumed her father was Japanese and her mother Italian. Otherwise, how could she talk such perfect Italian? She even had a slight Neapolitan inflexion. I had no idea if she'd been born in Italy or Japan. And that dark complexion must have come from her mother, as the Japanese are usually light-skinned.

"Good afternoon, Avvocato."

"Good afternoon. Please sit down."

I found my own voice a bit over-emphatic, and that made me feel uncomfortable.

This time Natsu took off her coat, sat down, and even smiled a little. The same perfume as last time already hung in the air.

"I'm pleased you've accepted the case. Fabio was really keen on getting you. He says that in prison . . ."

I felt a slight irritation. I didn't want her to continue. I didn't want her to tell me how much faith Fabio Rayban had in me. I didn't want her to remind me that I had decided to defend him for a reason he wouldn't like and I couldn't confess. So I made a gesture with my hand, as if to say, forget about that, I'm modest, I don't like compliments. The gesture was a lie: I actually like compliments a lot.

"As I said, it's just the way I work. I always like to look through the papers first to make sure there isn't any reason for me not to take on a case."

Why was I still talking such bullshit?

To put on airs, obviously. To play a part. To make myself look good. I was behaving like a schoolboy.

"What did you think when you read the file?"

"Pretty much what I'd thought before. This is a very difficult situation. Even supposing —"

I broke off, but too late. I was about to say, even supposing your husband is telling the truth – and supposing doesn't mean conceding – proving it, or at least creating a reasonable doubt, will be extremely difficult. I broke off because I didn't want to reawaken *her* more than reasonable doubts. But she understood.

"You mean: even supposing Fabio's story is true?"

I nodded, lowering my eyes. It seemed as if she wanted to say something else, but whatever it was she obviously decided not to say it. So it was up to me to continue.

"To try and get an acquittal, we'd have to prove that the drugs weren't your husband's. Or at the very least present arguments to the court that cast doubt on the idea that the drugs were your husband's."

"That means we would have to discover who planted them."

"Precisely. And as the whole thing happened in Montenegro a year and a half ago, I'm sure you realize —"

"That there's nothing we can do. Is that it?"

Well, I replied, it was true that there wasn't a lot we could do. But we could try to reconstruct, in as much detail as possible, what had happened in the days immediately prior to her husband being arrested. I told her, in a nutshell, what

Tancredi had suggested – making it seem as if everything was my idea. I spoke in the tones of someone who's used to this kind of investigation. As if all this was quite normal in my line of work.

When I'd finished explaining my plans for the investigation, she seemed impressed.

Damn, I was clearly someone who knew his stuff.

She asked if I wanted to start reconstructing the facts right now with her. I told her I preferred to talk to her husband first: I would visit him the next day, and then we two could meet before the end of the week.

She said that was fine. She asked me about the advance, I mentioned a figure, and when she took out a chequebook I asked her to see my secretary about that side of things. We princes of the bar don't dirty our hands with money or cheques.

That was all for the moment.

When she had gone I felt quite good, like someone who's made a good impression on the right person. I studiously avoided thinking about the implications of that.

9

Now I needed information about this Macrì.

The first thing I did was switch on my computer, go to the website of the bar association of Rome, and type in his name. What came up was the small amount of information most bar associations provide. Born in 1965, Macrì had been a member of the Rome association for just over three years and had previously been a member of the association in Reggio Calabria. His office was in a street with an unusual name. And it didn't have a phone. Where the contact details should have been, there was only a mobile number. Strange, I thought. A lawyer's office without a phone. I made a mental note of the fact. It might mean something.

I'd have to turn to some of my Roman friends if I wanted to find out more. So I went through the list of my so-called friends in Rome. It wasn't a long list.

There were a couple of colleagues I'd sometimes joined forces with for appeals to the Supreme Court or other proceedings that had gone through the Roman courts. To call them friends would have been an exaggeration. There was a journalist who had worked in Bari for some years on the legal column of *La Repubblica*. He was a pleasant guy, and we'd sometimes had a coffee or an aperitif together, but we'd never been more than casual acquaintances. And if I called him and asked him for information about Macrì, there was always the danger I'd arouse his professional curiosity.

There remained my old friend from university, Andrea Colaianni, an assistant prosecutor in the regional anti-Mafia department in Rome. The only person I could turn to without any hassle and who might be able to give me the information I needed.

I looked in my mobile's phonebook and found his number. For a few minutes I stared at the coloured screen. How long was it since Colaianni and I had last spoken? It must have been years. We'd run into each other once in the street in Bari when he was visiting his parents. We'd exchanged a few words and I'd had the impression that our friendship, like so many others, was over. Now I was phoning him – assuming the number was still valid. What would he think? What should I say to him? Should I chat for a while to observe the social conventions before I asked him for help?

I've always had major problems with telephones and telephone calls. What if he was annoyed? He might be in the middle of interrogating someone, or busy in some other way. Besides, magistrates – even if they're your friends – are unpredictable creatures.

OK. That's enough.

I pressed the button. Colaianni replied after two rings.

"Guido Guerrieri!" I was surprised he had my number in his phonebook.

"Hi, Andrea. How's it going?"

"Fine. And you?"

We started chatting. We chatted for at least ten minutes about various things. Family – well, his, at least – work, mutual friends neither of us had seen or heard from for ages. Sport. Did I still box? You're crazy as ever, Guerrieri.

Finally I told him the reason for my call. I explained everything, briefly. I told him I was groping in the dark, that

I didn't know what to do or what to tell my client. That I needed some information to help me see more clearly. Even if in the end it meant telling my client that the only serious prospect was to plea-bargain.

Colaianni told me he'd never heard of Macrì, though in a place like Rome that didn't mean anything. But he would ask around, and get back to me in a few days.

"But don't build up your hopes. The likeliest hypothesis is that your client really was transporting those drugs, but hadn't told his wife. The reason he denies it, despite all the evidence, is because he's ashamed and doesn't have the courage to admit it to her."

Right. I knew that and almost hoped that things really were like that.

It would all be so much simpler.

10

It had to happen sooner or later. I mean: that I would ask myself that question again. It happened quite naturally as I sat waiting for Paolicelli in the lawyers' room at the prison.

Were the rumours that had circulated in those days true? Was he really one of the people responsible for the death of that young man? Or at the very least, did he belong to the same gang as the killers?

For many months after that murder, I had been haunted by the image, created in my own troubled imagination, of Paolicelli watching that young man die with the same thin, evil smile I'd seen on his face while his Fascist friend had been beating me up.

At times it had occurred to me that I'd been lucky, because those guys were really crazy. I could easily have been stabbed to death myself, that evening I'd been beaten up because of my anorak.

For a long time I was obsessed with the idea of revenge. When I was older, stronger and, above all, knew how to fight – I'd already started learning to box – I would go and get them one by one and we'd settle our scores. The short, muscular one first, then the others, even though I didn't remember their faces very well, but that was a mere detail. Last but not least, the blond guy with the face like David Bowie, who'd smiled as he watched the show. And maybe while I beat him to a pulp, I'd also get him to tell me what had really happened on the evening of November the 28th, who the killers were and if he was one of them.

"Good morning, Avvocato."

I was so lost in thought that I hadn't even heard the door open. I nearly jumped, but managed to control it. I replied, with a slight change of facial expression. That was as friendly as I was prepared to be to Paolicelli after that flood of memories.

"I'm very pleased you've taken on my case. It gives me the feeling there's a real possibility now. My wife also told me you inspire confidence."

I felt ill at ease when he mentioned his wife. And the other thing that made me ill at ease was that he was so different from the evil-faced young man I'd hated all through my teenage years. He was a normal person, almost likeable.

But I didn't want him to be likeable.

"Signor Paolicelli, I think we should be clear about something right from the start. So that you don't have any unrealistic expectations. I've decided to accept your case and I'll do whatever I can for you. We'll decide together on our strategy and on what we choose to do in court, but what you have to know, what you have to be absolutely aware of, is that you're still in a very difficult situation."

It was a good way of approaching things. The technical tone I was adopting helped to dispel the embarrassment I had felt a few moments earlier. And behind my front of professional efficiency, I was actually being pretty nasty to him. I'd immediately deprived him of even that momentary relief, that comfort felt by anyone who, after months of prison and gloomy forebodings about the future, meets someone who is on his side and can help him.

The very reason, basically, for the existence of lawyers.

You're really an arsehole, Guerrieri, I told myself.

I opened my briefcase to take out the papers, and started speaking again without even looking at him. "I've been through all the documents, made a few notes, and now I'm here to discuss what line we take. There are basically two options. Both very different."

I looked up to make sure he was following me. It was the first time I'd looked him in the face and seen it the way it really was: the lined face of a man in his forties with curiously gentle blue eyes, not the face that had been embedded in my memory all these years, the face of a teenage Fascist with an evil smile.

It was a very strange, very confusing feeling. Things weren't right, weren't as I'd expected.

Paolicelli nodded, because I'd stopped speaking and he wanted to know which two options we had, *basically*.

"As I was saying, there are two options. The first is damage limitation. That means we go to the appeal court, hope we have an assistant prosecutor who's flexible, and we plea-bargain and try to get the largest reduction we can in your sentence . . ."

He was about to interrupt me but I raised my hand to stop him, as if to say, wait, let me finish.

"I know what you're going to say. The drugs weren't yours. I know, but right now I have to present you with the different options, and what each entails. Then you'll decide what to do. So, as I was saying, that's the first option. With a little luck we could bring the sentence down to ten years, perhaps even less, which means —"

"My wife said you thought we could make some inquiries. To find out who put the cocaine in the car."

Why did it bother me that he was constantly mentioning

his wife? Why did it bother me that his wife had talked to him about our conversations? I asked myself these questions and didn't wait for the answers. They were too obvious to need putting into words.

"We could try."

"In order to get an acquittal?"

"In order to get an acquittal. But we have to be clear about this. There's no guarantee we'll find anything. In fact it's very unlikely. We'll talk now and see if we come up with anything useful. But even if we can construct a specific hypothesis as to how those drugs ended up in your car, our real problem is convincing the court of appeal. And we certainly won't do that if all we have is conjecture."

"What do you want to know?"

I repeated the lesson Tancredi had taught me. "Did you meet anyone during your holiday? I mean, someone who was very friendly, maybe even too friendly. Someone who asked questions, tried to find out where you were from, when you were leaving."

He waited a moment before replying. "No. We did meet people, of course, but we didn't make any friends. We didn't hang around with the people we happened to meet."

"No one asked you when you were leaving?"

Once again he didn't reply immediately. He was making an effort to see if he could remember anything useful, but in the end had to give up.

"All right, it doesn't matter. Let's talk about the hotel car park."

"As I told you, we gave the keys to the porter because the car park was small and always full. A lot of cars were double parked and they needed the keys to move them."

"And did that happen the night before you left, too?"

"Yes, every night we left the keys in the porter's lodge. In the morning, if we wanted to go for a drive, we'd pick them up. If not they stayed there all day."

"Was there only one porter?"

"No, there were three of them on shifts, day and night."

"Do you remember which of the three was on duty the last night you were there?"

No, he didn't remember. He'd already thought about this, he said, and had never managed to pin down which man he had left his keys with the last time.

It was a blind alley. Both of us fell silent.

In my mind, I worked out what might have happened, always supposing that Paolicelli wasn't having me and his wife on.

During the night, these people had taken the car to a safe place somewhere. A machine shop, a garage, or maybe just an isolated spot in the country. There, they had filled it with drugs and then had brought it back to the hotel car park. Easy and safe, with very few risks.

In any case, we wouldn't get very far pursuing the business of the porters, since we had no evidence as to which of the three – supposing one of the three was really involved – had been part of the operation.

And even if we could, what then? What would I do? Call Interpol and ask them to launch an international investigation to clear my client? I told myself we were just wasting time. Innocent or guilty, Paolicelli was in it up to his neck. The only sensible thing I could do as a professional was limit the damage as much as possible.

I asked him if he had noticed anyone on the ferry who he'd already seen in Montenegro, either in the hotel or anywhere else.

"Yes, there was someone on the ferry who'd been in our hotel. He's the only one I remember."

"Do you remember where he was from, what his name was?"

Paolicelli shook his head firmly. "It's not that I don't remember. I just don't know. I'd seen him a few times in the hotel. Then I saw him again for a moment on the ferry and we waved at each other. That was it. The only thing I know is that he was Italian."

"But would you recognize him if you saw him again?"

"Yes, I think so. I remember him quite well. But how do we trace him?"

I replied with a gesture of the hand which was supposed to mean: don't worry. I know what to do, this is my job. When the moment comes, we'll manage. Which was mostly nonsense, of course. It wasn't my job at all – it was the police who traced people, not lawyers – and anyway, I had no idea what to do. Apart from going back to Tancredi and asking for his help.

To Paolicelli, though, that gesture of mine seemed to be all he needed. If you know what to do and this is your job, then I'm calm. I chose the right lawyer, the one who'll get me out of this. The Perry Mason of the Murgia.

That would do for this morning, I thought.

He realized the interview was over. I was about to leave and he was about to go back to his cell. But I could tell from his face that he didn't want to be alone again.

"I'm sorry, Avvocato, I have another question. You said we could either plea-bargain or decide to appeal. When do we have to decide? I mean, what's the last moment we can leave it till?"

"The day of the hearing. That's when we have to say if we

intend to plea-bargain, which would bring proceedings to an end, or if we want to carry on. It's a few weeks yet before the hearing, so we have time to think about it, and to see if we can find out anything useful. If we don't, then any option other than plea-bargaining would be suicidal."

There wasn't much to add, and we both knew it. He looked away from me and fixed his gaze on the floor. After a while he started to wring his hands methodically, so hard that he seemed about to dislocate them.

I was about to stand up, say goodbye and leave. I could feel my leg muscles impelling me to get to my feet and get away from the chair, away from that place.

But I didn't move. I thought he was entitled to a few minutes' silence. To give free rein to his despair, in his own time. To wring his hands without having me interrupt him to say that we'd finished for the day, that I was leaving – leaving a place he couldn't leave – and that we'd meet again soon.

When I decide, of course, not when you decide.

Because I'm free and you're not.

He was entitled to those few minutes of silence in my company, to go off in pursuit of his own thoughts.

To fill the time, I also gave myself up to my thoughts. Once again, I thought about the situation we were in. I was aware of it, and he wasn't. I knew we'd met all those years before, he didn't. In a sense he'd never known it, because in all probability he hadn't even looked properly at the face of the boy his friend had beaten up. Besides, he'd almost certainly forgotten all about it.

So he had no idea he had been an obsession of mine all through my teenage years.

He had no idea that, in my waking dreams of revenge, I'd often smashed his friend's face in first, and then his. He had no idea, and now I was his lawyer, in other words his only hope.

He continued wringing his hands. I recalled the speech I had imagined myself making when the moment came.

Do you remember when you and your friends beat and humiliated that young boy who didn't want to take off his anorak? Do you remember? That bastard friend of yours smashed his face in and you watched and smiled smugly. Well, I was that boy and now I'm here to smash your face in. You won't look like a David Bowie of the suburbs any more and our account will finally be settled.

Or rather, no, before settling our account you have to tell me if it was you who stabbed that other boy. Did you hold the knife, and then sacrifice the poor bastard who killed himself in prison? And if you didn't actually hold the knife in your hand, were you part of the gang? Tell me, damn it.

I noticed that he was clenching his fists under the desk.

Then he thanked me. For being so frank with him, and so fair. He said he was sure that if there was a way out, I would find it.

Then he said something else. "You realized that I needed to get it out of my system and you didn't interrupt me, didn't say you had to go. You're a good man."

As I left the prison, these words were still clattering around in my head.

I was a good man.

Of course I was.

11

The next day I called Tancredi again and told him about my conversation with Paolicelli in the prison.

He listened without saying a word until I'd finished.

"As I told you last time, if you wanted to identify the hotel staff, there'd have to be an ongoing official investigation. If there was, then we could go through Interpol and let the police in Podgorica fuck us around officially."

"I was thinking about the man on the ferry. The one who was in the same hotel as Paolicelli, the one he saw again on the return crossing."

"And what do you suggest we do? Oh, yes, the passenger list. We trace all the male passengers on that ferry – only a few hundred at most – and then we get hold of their photographs and take them to your client in prison. Look, is it this one? No? What about this one? No, it's that one! Bingo! We've identified a dangerous tourist we can charge with aggravated international travel. You've practically won the case."

"Carmelo, listen to me. I know perfectly well we're not going to get anywhere with the people in the hotel or with what happened in Montenegro in general. But I must tell you this: the more I think about it, the stronger the feeling I have that Paolicelli is telling the truth. I know intuition and all that is mostly bullshit, but I talked to him and the way he tells it, the look on his face, everything —"

"Let me introduce Guido Guerrieri. No one can ever tell him a lie."

But there wasn't much conviction in his voice. It was a last skirmish. Carmelo knew I didn't easily go overboard for my clients.

"All right, what would you like us to do?"

"The passenger list, Carmelo. Get hold of it, narrow it down to the Italian citizens – Paolicelli said the man was Italian – and then check your database to see if any of these people have a record for drug trafficking."

I could just see him shaking his head. He said it would take him at least a day, he would have to waste one of his days off, and it wouldn't lead anywhere anyway, but in the end he took the details of the boat and the crossing.

"After this, Guerrieri, you'll be in debt to me your whole life." And he hung up.

*

I spent the whole afternoon preparing my opening argument for a case due to be heard the following morning.

I was representing an association of people who lived a few hundred yards from a waste disposal plant. When the wind was blowing the wrong way – in other words, from the plant to the built-up area where they lived – the smell was revolting.

The delegates of the association had come to my office and explained the situation. Before they would agree to entrust me with the case, they had demanded that I take a little trip to where they lived so that I could be made directly aware of the nature of the problem.

As I entered the home of the association's chairman, I could sense something slightly nauseous in the background.

A smell that suggested something mysterious, unnameable, hidden in that apparently normal dwelling. The man asked me to follow him into the kitchen and sit down, and his wife made coffee.

After a while, I had the impression that the chairman, his wife and the other members of the association were exchanging knowing glances. As if to say, now we'll show him.

They're a Satanic sect, I told myself. Someone's going to come up behind me now and hit me on the head. Then they'll take me to a garage equipped for sabbaths and black masses and cut me in pieces with ceremonial knives acquired at the local discount store. Maybe before that, they'll force me to have ritual sex with this priestess of Mephistopheles here. I looked at the chairman's wife – five feet tall, weighing about twelve stone, a pleasant face and a moustache like a pirate – and told myself this would probably be the most Satanic part of the whole thing.

The chairman's wife served the coffee and we drank in silence.

Then, without a word, they opened the window, and in a few seconds the air was filled with a smell so thick you could almost touch it. It was a mixture of rotten eggs and ammonia, with a strong pinch of essence of putrefying wild animal.

The chairman asked me if I understood their problem. I said yes, I understood it a whole lot better now. If they would excuse me, I really had to run – literally *run* – but they could rest assured I would give the case the attention it deserved. And I meant it.

They were very persuasive, I thought as I returned to my office. The smell was still on my clothes and in my stomach, and I knew it wouldn't go away any time soon.

12

When I'd finished preparing my argument and had only a few details left to check, I told Maria Teresa to phone Signora Kawabata and ask her if she could come to the office some time in the week, because I needed to talk to her.

Officially because I wanted to hear her version of what had happened during the last days of the holiday, and on the ferry crossing, and all the rest of it.

Maria Teresa came back a few minutes later. She had Signora Kawabata on the line. She could even come now if that was all right with me.

I pretended to think it over for a few seconds, then said yes, all right, we could do it now.

When Maria Teresa had gone out again, I went to the washroom. I tried as best I could to wipe from my face all signs of the hours I'd spent studying reports by expert chemists and statements from environmental groups. I washed my face, combed my hair, pinched my cheeks a few times to get some colour back into them, and after a brief hesitation put on a little of the scent I kept in the office and had hardly used. Not since Margherita had left anyway.

As I came out of the washroom it struck me that I might have overdone the scent and was going to look really stupid, at least to Maria Teresa. She was sure to figure out what was going on if she came back into my room and it smelled like an employment agency for gigolos.

I tried to get back to work, with non-existent success. I twice opened and closed a book of environmental regulations, leafed through the file, finally put on a CD, and even before the music started switched off the stereo. Again, I thought Maria Teresa might be suspicious, might imagine I'd put on the music to create a mood or something like that.

In the end I settled down, sitting on the edge of my swivel chair, my elbows propped on the desk, my chin propped on my hands, my eyes on the door.

Finally I heard the buzz of the entryphone. Then I noticed that the desk was untidy and tried to clear away a few papers and arrange some of the books in piles. When I heard the office doorbell ring I sat down again, pinched my face a few more times, and assumed a casual posture. If you could call it that.

By the time Maria Teresa came in to announce Signora – it seemed to me she emphasized the word – Kawabata, I'd turned into a third-rate imitation of the main character from *Play It Again, Sam*. The only thing I hadn't done was scatter a few books of philosophy around, just to look like an intellectual.

Natsu entered. With her, holding her left hand, was a little girl. She had her mother's face: the same cheeks, the same mouth, the same colouring, more Vietnamese than Japanese. And amid all that, her father's blue eyes.

She was very beautiful.

The moment I saw her, I felt an acute, incomprehensible twinge of nostalgia.

"This is Anna Midori," Natsu said, smiling slightly. Because of the look on my face, I imagine. Then she turned to her daughter. "And this . . ." She hesitated for a moment.

"Guido, my name's Guido," I said, walking around the

66

desk, trying to give the kind of smile that meant, I'm used to dealing with children.

I was a complete idiot.

Anna Midori held out her hand solemnly, and looked at me with those incredible blue eyes.

"How old are you?" I asked, holding her hand in mine.

"Six. And you?"

For a moment I was tempted to shave a few years off my age. "Forty-two."

This was followed by a few seconds of embarrassed silence. Natsu was the first to speak.

"Do you think we could leave Anna with your secretary for a few minutes?"

I thought we could. I called Maria Teresa and asked her if she'd mind keeping an eye on this lovely child for a bit.

This lovely child. Why was I talking this way? I was about to introduce them, but Maria Teresa interrupted me.

"Oh, Anna and I already know each other. We were just introduced, weren't we, Anna? Anna Midori."

"Yes. We have the same eyes."

It was true. Maria Teresa wasn't a particularly pretty girl, but she had amazing eyes. Blue, like Anna Midori's. And Fabio Paolicelli's.

"Come on, Anna. I'll show you a game on my computer."

The girl turned to her mother, who nodded. Maria Teresa took her hand and they went out.

"Are you really forty-two?"

"Yes. Why?"

"You don't . . . you don't look it."

I resisted the impulse to ask her how old I looked and told her to take a seat. I walked back behind my desk and sat down.

"Your daughter is . . . very beautiful. I've never seen such a beautiful little girl."

Natsu smiled. "Do you have children?"

The question took me by surprise. "No."

"Aren't you married?"

"Well, that's rather a long story . . ."

"I'm sorry. I always ask too many questions. It's a failing of mine."

No, don't say that, it doesn't matter. If you want me to, I'll tell you my life story and then you can tell me yours. It'll be better than talking about work. Which would mean talking about your *husband*.

Damn it, what was I getting myself into?

I shook my head politely. It's no problem, really.

"We're trying to figure out who put the drugs in your car and how. It seems very likely that it happened when the car was in the hotel car park. Do you remember the name of the porter on duty the last night?"

She didn't remember. She was usually a bit distracted and didn't pay much attention to people.

She would obviously be a great help in our so-called investigation.

"Apart from the porter, did you notice anything unusual during your stay or during the return journey? When you were on the ferry, did you see anyone you'd already seen during the holiday, staying at the same hotel?"

She hadn't noticed anything. She hadn't even noticed the man who'd stayed at their hotel and then had travelled back on the same ferry. She told me her husband, when he'd talked to her about our conversation, had already mentioned this man and had asked her if she remembered him.

But she didn't remember him, probably because she hadn't really seen him.

I kept going with my questions a while longer, trying to get her to remember something, anything. Even details which seemed insignificant, I said, could turn out to be very useful. This was the way an investigator had to proceed, it seemed to me. In fact I had no idea what I was doing and was basically just imitating what detectives did in crime movies.

In the end I gave up. But I told her to think about it later and, if she remembered anything, even that famous apparently insignificant detail, to call me.

As I said this, I had a sudden feeling of pointlessness. Mixed with shame. This investigation of mine was a farce. I wouldn't find out anything. I was just trying to impress Natsu. I was unfairly deluding her and her bastard of a husband.

I told myself I should finish with this nonsense as soon as possible. I would wait to see what Colaianni told me about Macrì and what Tancredi came up with on the subject of the passenger list and then, since it was highly unlikely anything would come of it, I would talk to Paolicelli and tell him that unfortunately we had no choice but to plea-bargain.

I would say that I realized how difficult it was to agree to something like that, if you think you're innocent – if you *are* innocent – but unfortunately we had to be realistic. With no evidence in our favour, nothing that could be used to introduce a degree of reasonable doubt, it would be madness to give up on plea-bargaining and go ahead with an appeal. We had to limit the damage.

I stood up, and after a moment's hesitation she stood up, too.

"You told me you'd like to try my cooking."

"I'm sorry?"

"There's an exhibition opening tomorrow night." She took a small card made from rough white paper out of her handbag. "There's a reception and I'm taking care of the buffet. Japanese food with a few variants of my own creation."

She handed me the card.

"This is an invitation for two. You can bring your girlfriend if you like, or whoever. The reception starts at nine o'clock. I think it could be fun. It's in a garage that's been converted into an exhibition space."

I thanked her and looked at the card. I had never heard of either the artist – nothing unusual about that – or the address. And that was a little more unusual, as it was in Bari.

I told her I had a previous engagement, but I'd see if I could get out of it because I'd really like to go.

Of course I didn't have any previous engagement. I'd only said that to make myself look good. Don't worry about me, I have a wild social life. I'm not a loser who spends his evenings in the office studying files, or in a gym taking punches, or alone at the cinema, trying not to think about his girlfriend who left him.

A stab of pain. A photographic negative of Margherita. Dissolve.

Now Natsu really had to go. She walked a little faster to the door, as if she felt embarrassed and wanted to leave in order to get rid of that embarrassment.

We shook hands, and I opened the door for her. The little girl was sitting on Maria Teresa's lap at the computer, which was emitting strange gurgling and splashing sounds.

The girl asked when she could come back and play Bubbles and Splashes again. Maria Teresa told her she could come back whenever she liked, and the girl kissed her, jumped up and went to her mummy. On the way out, she even waved goodbye to me.

"Beautiful little girl, isn't she?" I said when they had gone.

"Beautiful?" Maria Teresa replied. "She's amazing."

"Yes, she's very beautiful," I said, as I went back into my room, lost in thought.

I went and sat down, and stayed there for at least five minutes, without doing or saying anything.

When I came to my senses, I got out the street map to look for that address.

13

In front of the entrance stood a man who looked like a bodybuilder. He was wearing a dark suit, and had a microphone and earpiece. He asked me if I was alone. No, I'm with the invisible woman. And from the intelligent look on your face, I assume you're Ben Grimm.

I didn't say that, but I did go right up to him – wondering who'd emerge the winner if we got into a fight – and made a gesture with my hand, to show him that there was no one next to me, so yes, I was alone. It didn't occur to me to say it out loud.

He let me pass, and then whispered a few words I didn't catch into the microphone. Maybe he was warning his colleagues inside that a suspicious character was coming in and they'd better keep an eye on him. I descended a ramp and found myself in a strange place. It was a real garage, though obviously without cars. The floor was covered with porphyry building blocks, and scattered throughout the space were those mushroom-shaped heaters you find in bars so that people can be in the open air even in winter. It was fairly cold all the same, so although I unbuttoned my jacket I didn't take it off.

There were a lot of people there. My first thought, as I entered, was that it was like some vaguely surreal film set. Groups of very well-to-do but left-wing ladies. Groups of unmistakably gay young men and women. Groups of people of different ages, dressed to display the fact that they were artists. A few politicians, a few would-be intellectuals, a few young black men, a few Japanese. No one I knew.

It was such a weird mixture that it immediately put me in a good mood. I thought I would take a quick look at the works, in order not to be unprepared, and then look for the food. And Natsu.

On a small table, close to the entrance, there were catalogues. I took one and leafed through it as I moved closer to the walls. The title of the exhibition was *The Elementary Particles*.

I wondered if it was a reference to the novel by that Frenchman. I hadn't liked the book, but I assumed it was meant to be a clue to understanding the works.

From a distance, the paintings on display were reminiscent of Rothko. All things considered, they weren't bad. I went up to one of them. I was examining it, trying to grasp the technique, when a voice behind me made me jump.

"Are you Piero's boyfriend?" He had orange hair and looked like an Elton John clone. A local Elton John, judging by the accent.

No, friend, you're more likely to be Piero's boyfriend, whoever the hell this Piero is.

"No, I'm afraid you've made a mistake. You must be confusing me with someone else."

"Oh," he said, with a sigh that could mean anything. Then he looked me up and down and asked, "Do you like Katso's work?"

"Who?"

Katso was the artist, it turned out. Elton explained that he had thought up the title of the exhibition and had written the critical introduction to the catalogue.

Oh, excellent. I'd glanced at it and hadn't understood a word.

I didn't say that, but he read my mind, and without my asking started to explain his introduction in detail.

I couldn't believe it. There were at least two hundred people there, and this character had buttonholed me. I'd have liked to signal to someone to come and save me, maybe by knocking Elton on the head, but I didn't know anyone.

After a while I noticed that people were moving in groups towards the side of the garage furthest from the entrance. The movement you always get at parties when the food is ready.

"I think there's something to eat," I said, but he didn't even hear me.

He was unstoppable now, having launched on a metaphysical exegesis on the works of Katso.

"Spudlicating, humbo," I said. Complete gibberish, just to make sure he wasn't listening to a word I said. And it was true: he really wasn't. He didn't ask me what "spudlicating" meant, or even what a "humbo" was. He was too busy talking about archetypes and the way certain artistic manifestations condensed the scattered fragments of the collective unconscious.

I condensed *my* scattered fragments and said excuse me – only because I'm such a polite person – turned and headed towards the food.

People were crowding around a long table. From a room immediately behind it, waiters emerged with trays full of sushi, sashimi and tempura. At one end of the table were wooden chopsticks wrapped in paper, at the other, plastic knives and forks for the inexperienced.

I made my way between the people without bothering

too much about the queue, filled a plate, poured a lot of soy sauce over it, took a pair of chopsticks and went and sat down on a stool away from the others, to eat in peace.

The food was very good. It had clearly been prepared there, just before being served, not frozen and kept for hours in a fridge, and I enjoyed it more than anything I'd eaten for quite a while. A waiter passed with a tray of glasses filled with white wine. I took two, mumbling that I was expecting a lady. The wine wasn't as good as the food, but at least it was nice and cold. I drank the first glass straight down and disposed of it under the stool, then sipped in a more civilized manner at the second. Gradually the crowd around the table dispersed.

It was then that Natsu emerged from the room behind the table. She was in a white chef's uniform, which set off her dark complexion and black hair spectacularly.

She glanced at the table, which looked as if a swarm of locusts had passed over it. Then she looked around and I stood up without even realizing it. After a few moments, our eyes met. I waved awkwardly. She smiled and came towards me.

"Good evening."

"Good evening."

There were a few seconds of embarrassment. I felt the impulse to say that the food was very good, that she was an exceptionally good cook, and other highly original remarks like that. Fortunately, I managed to restrain myself.

"I could do with a cigarette. Do you mind going outside with me?"

I said I didn't mind at all and we walked together towards the entrance, where all the smokers had gathered. She took out a packet of blue Chesterfields, and offered me one. I said no, thanks. She took one for herself and lit it.

"How long is it since you quit smoking?"

"How do you know I quit?"

"The way you looked at the packet. I know that look because I quit a few times myself. What do you think of the show?"

"Interesting. I didn't understand the catalogue at all, and I didn't understand very much of the works. Then an Elton John lookalike who talked like the comedian Lino Banfi asked me if I was Piero's boyfriend and —"

She burst out laughing. Loudly, with real gusto, which surprised me because I didn't think I'd been that funny.

"I didn't think you were so nice when I saw you at work." She laughed again. "You were like one of those lawyers in American films, the efficient, ruthless kind."

Efficient and ruthless. I liked that. I'd have preferred "handsome and ruthless", like Tommy Lee Jones in *The Fugitive*, but I didn't mind.

She smoked a little more.

"Did you come by car?"

No, of course not, we're only five or six miles from the centre of town. Every evening I train for the New York Marathon. I ran all the way here, in jumpsuit and track shoes, and changed before I came in.

"Yes, of course."

"I've finished here. I haven't got a car, I came in the van with my colleagues. You could give me a lift home, if you like."

Yes, I'd like that, I said, trying to hide my surprise. She told me to give her five minutes, which was how long it would take her to get out of her work uniform, give instructions to her colleagues about clearing everything away, and say goodbye to the organizers of the evening.

I stood and waited for her at the entrance, with the bodybuilder for company. Every now and again he'd whisper something into his microphone, his bovine eyes busy staring into the depths of nothingness.

Almost a quarter of an hour went by. People came in and out. I should have asked myself what I was doing. I mean, Natsu was the wife of a client of mine who was in prison. I shouldn't have been here. But I had no desire to ask myself that question.

Natsu came out again. Even in the semi-darkness I noticed that she had spent part of those fifteen minutes doing her make-up and hair.

"Shall we go?" she said.

"Let's go," I replied.

14

We drove quickly to the ring road. As we moved onto the ramp, the electronic notes of 'Boulevard of Broken Dreams' by Green Day came from the CD player.

I told myself I was a fool and a hothead. I was over forty – well over forty – and I was behaving recklessly and like a bastard.

Take her home now, say goodnight politely, then go home yourself and go to bed.

"Shall we go for a drive?" I said.

She did not reply immediately, as if she was undecided. Then she looked at her watch.

"I don't have much time, half an hour at the most. I promised the babysitter I'd be home by one. She's a student and she has classes tomorrow."

Did you get that? She has to go home to her little girl, because, you idiot, she's a married woman, with a daughter, and a husband in prison. And in case you've forgotten, her husband is your client. Now take her home and let that be the end of it.

"Of course, of course, I just thought . . . we could go for a drive, listen to some music . . . Anyway, I'm sorry, I'll take you home now, you'll be there in no time . . . Just tell me the address —"

"Listen," she said, interrupting me, talking quickly, "this is what we can do, if you like. We go to my place, you drop me and drive around for ten minutes. I pay the babysitter, she leaves, and you come up for a drink and a little chat. What do you say?"

I didn't reply immediately because I couldn't swallow. My moral dilemmas were swept away like the dirt in those commercials for sink cleaners. Yes, I said, that'd be great. We could have a drink and a chat.

And maybe a kiss and a cuddle and a fuck.

And then repent at leisure.

We reached her place, which was in Poggiofranco. An apartment block with a garden, the kind we used to envy when we were children, because the kids my age who lived in places like that could go down and play football whenever they liked, without their parents saying anything.

In the Seventies, Poggiofranco had been known as something of a Fascist stronghold, certainly not a place where a child from a left-wing family would have gone. It struck me that their apartment may have been where Paolicelli had lived as a boy. It was an unsettling thought and I dismissed it immediately.

Before she got out of the car, Natsu asked me for my mobile number. "I'll call you in ten minutes," she said, and was gone.

I went and parked a couple of streets further on. I switched off the radio and sat there, in silence, enjoying the forbidden, intoxicating sense of anticipation. Just over fifteen minutes later – I had looked at my watch at least ten times – my mobile phone rang. She told me I could come now if I wanted to. Yes, I did want to, I said to myself after ringing off. I left the car where I had parked it, walked a few hundred yards, and in five minutes I was back at the apartment building. When I reached the landing, I found Natsu waiting for me. She let me in and quickly closed the door.

The apartment had the characteristic smell of places where there are children. I hadn't been to many but the smell was unmistakable. A mixture of talcum powder, milk, a hint of fruit and a few other things. Natsu led me to the kitchen. It was a large, warm, cheerful room with wooden furniture hand-varnished in yellow and orange. I told her I really liked the furniture and she replied that she had varnished all of it herself.

In the kitchen, the smell of children was less obvious, covered by the nice smells of food. I remember thinking how good this apartment smelled, and then I wondered what the bedroom was like, and what it smelled like. I immediately felt ashamed and forced myself to think about something else.

Natsu put on a CD. *Feels Like Home* by Norah Jones. At low volume, so as not to wake the little girl.

She asked me what I wanted to drink and I said I wouldn't mind a little rum if she had any. She took a bottle of Jamaican rum from a cupboard and poured some into two large, thick glasses.

We were sitting at an orange-varnished wooden table. As we talked, I touched the surface of the table with my fingertips. I liked the touch of it, rough and smooth at the same time, and the bright orange colour. Everything in that kitchen gave me a feeling of sweet-smelling, light-filled solidity.

"You do know I came to watch you in court, just before Fabio appointed you?"

For some reason, I thought for a moment of saying, no, I didn't know. Then I thought better of it.

"Yes, I saw you."

"Ah. I thought that our eyes met once, but I wasn't sure."

"How did you come to be there?"

"Fabio told me he wanted to appoint you, so I thought I'd

go and see if you were really as good as they'd told him you were."

"And how did you know I was going to be in court that day?"

"I didn't. I'd been going to the courthouse for a few days, walking past the courtrooms and asking people if anyone had seen a lawyer called Guerrieri. Once you passed by just as I was asking someone, and he was going to call you. I had to stop him. Then finally, they told me you were in court that morning, and your trial was just starting. So I went in and sat in on the whole hearing. And I thought you were as good as they said."

I didn't think I could hide my childish smugness and so I decided to change the subject.

"Do you mind my asking where your accent comes from?"

Before answering, she opened the window, emptied her glass and took out a cigarette. Did I mind if she smoked? No, I didn't mind. Which was both true and false.

Her father, as I'd thought, was Japanese, and her mother from Naples. Her name was actually Maria Natsu, but no one had ever called her that. The name Maria only appeared on her papers, she said, and she paused for a few moments, as if this was something important that she'd only just become aware of.

Then she refilled our glasses and told me her story.

How she'd spent her childhood and adolescence partly in Rome, partly in Kyoto. How her parents had died in a road accident, while travelling. How she'd started work as a photographic and catwalk model. How she'd met Paolicelli in Milan.

"Fabio was part-owner of a dress showroom. I was twenty-three when we met. All the girls were crazy about him. I felt so privileged when he chose me. We got married a year later."

"What's the difference in age between you and him?"

"Eleven years."

"How on earth did you end up in Bari, after Milan?"

"For a few years, Fabio's work was going really well. Then things changed, I never understood why. I won't go into details, because it isn't a very amusing story, but his firm went bankrupt and in a few months we were completely penniless. That's when we decided to come to Bari, which is Fabio's home town. He was born here and lived here until he was nineteen. This apartment belonged to his parents and was available. So at least we wouldn't have to pay rent."

"Was that when you started working as a chef?"

"Yes. I'd learned to cook when I was young. My father had two restaurants in Rome. When we got to Bari we had to make a new life for ourselves. Fabio became the representative for some designers he'd known in Milan, and I found work at Placebo, where they needed a Japanese chef two evenings a week. Then they started to offer me work organizing dinners and receptions. That's my main job now. Apart from the restaurant, I'm busy at least eight or nine evenings a month."

"There's a lot of money in this city. To organize a reception like the one tonight must seem like a good way to show it off."

I was about to add that a lot of that money was of dubious provenance, to say the least. But then I remembered that her husband's money might not be all that legitimate either and I said nothing.

"What about you?"

"Me?"

"You live alone, right?"

"Yes."

"Have you always been alone? No wives or girlfriends?"

I made a noise that was meant to be a kind of bitter laugh. As if to say: *Nobody knows the trouble I've seen.*

"My wife left me some time ago. Or to be more precise, she told me she was leaving me some time ago."

"Why?"

"Many excellent reasons." I hoped she wouldn't ask me what these excellent reasons were. She didn't.

"And what happened after that?"

Yes. What had happened? I tried to tell her, leaving out the parts I hadn't really understood and the parts that were too painful. There were a lot of those. When I'd finished my story, it was her turn again, and that was how we got onto the subject of her ex-boyfriend Paolo and the game of wishes.

"Paolo was a painter. For some reason you remind me of him. Unfortunately, I wasn't in love with him." She paused, and for a few moments her eyes seemed to be searching for something that wasn't in the room. "He found a . . . a really beautiful way to tell me he liked me."

"What was it?"

"The game of coloured wishes. He said a girlfriend had shown it to him, a few years before. But I'm sure he made it up on the spot, just for me."

She paused again for a few moments, probably remembering other things that she didn't tell me. Instead she asked me if I wanted to play the game. I said I did, and she explained the rules.

"You make three wishes. You have to say two of them, the third one you can keep secret. For the wishes to come true, they must have a colour."

I half-closed my eyes and moved my head slightly towards her. Like someone who hasn't heard, or hasn't quite understood. "A colour?"

"Yes, it's one of the rules. The wishes can only come true if they're in colour."

For the wishes to come true, they must be in colour. Right. Now I knew why none of the wishes I'd made in my life had come true. There was this rule, and no one had told me.

"Tell me your wishes."

I can't usually answer questions about wishes. Either I can't or don't want to. Which comes to the same thing.

Confessing your wishes, your real wishes, even to yourself, is dangerous. If they can be realized, which they often can, stating them confronts you with your fear of trying. In other words, with your own cowardice. So you prefer not to think about them, or you tell yourself they're impossible, and grown-up people don't wish for impossible things.

That night I replied without hesitation. "When I was a little boy I used to say that I wanted to be a writer."

"All right. And what colour is that wish?"

"Blue, I'd say."

"What kind of blue?"

"Blue. I don't know."

She made an impatient gesture with her hand, like a schoolmistress dealing with a pupil who's a bit thick. Then she stood up, left the kitchen and came back a minute later, with a book called *The Great Atlas of Colours*.

"There are two hundred colours here. Now choose your wish."

She opened the book at the first page of the section on blues. There were lots and lots of little squares with the most incredible shades of blue. Under each one, a name. Some

I'd never heard of, and not knowing the names I hadn't even seen them. Things don't exist unless you have names for them, I thought, as I started to leaf through the pages.

Prussian blue, turquoise, slate, dark sky blue, Provençal lavender blue, topaz blue, cold blue, powder blue, baby blue, indigo, French marine, ink, Mediterranean blue, sapphire, royal blue, clear cyan, fleur-de-lys, and many others.

"You mustn't be approximate, otherwise your wishes won't come true. Choose the exact colour of your wish."

It only took me a few more seconds. "The exact colour is indigo," I said.

She nodded, as if it was the answer she had expected. The right answer.

"Second wish."

It was getting harder now, but again I didn't hesitate.

"I'd like to have a child. Right now I'd say that's a lot more unrealistic than the first wish."

She looked at me strangely. She didn't seem surprised, though. It was as if she'd expected that answer, too. "And what colour is it?"

I leafed through the book, then closed it. "Many, many colours."

This time she didn't insist on having me say the *exact colour* and didn't make any comment. I liked the fact that she didn't make any comment. I liked that naturalness, I liked the way everything seemed right, at that moment.

"The third one."

"You told me one of the wishes can be a secret."

"Yes."

"This is the secret one."

"All right. But you still have to tell me the colour, even if the wish is secret."

Right. The wish is secret, not the colour. OK. I took the atlas and opened it at the section on reds.

Wine, crimson, vermillion, powder rose, red rose petal, modern coral, neon red, cerise, terracotta, garnet, flame, ruby, academy red, rust, radicchio, dark red, port.

"Crimson. I'd say crimson. Now it's your turn."

"I want Anna Midori to be happy and free. And that wish is leaf green."

There was something in the way she said it that sent shivers down my spine.

"Then I'd like to know if Fabio is guilty or innocent. If he told me the truth or not. I'd like to know." She hesitated. "This desire to know is brown, but it changes shade constantly. Sometimes it's the colour of mahogany, sometimes it's like leather, or tea, or bitter chocolate. Sometimes it turns almost black." She looked me straight in the eyes.

"And the third one?"

"My third one's a secret, too."

"And what colour is it?"

She didn't say anything, but leafed through the atlas to the end of the section on reds. My heart started beating slightly faster.

Just then, we heard a prolonged, heart-rending scream. Natsu put down her glass and rushed to her daughter's room. I ran after her.

Midori was lying on her back, the sheets thrown off, the pillow on the floor. She had stopped screaming and was talking now in a laboured way, in an incomprehensible language, and trembling. Natsu put her hand on the girl's forehead and told her Mummy was here, but she didn't stop trembling, didn't open her eyes, and kept talking.

Not even realizing what I was doing, I took Midori's hand and said, "It's all right, sweetheart. Everything's all right."

It was like magic. The girl opened her eyes, without seeing us. There was a look of astonishment on her face. She trembled one more time, said a few more words in that mysterious language, but calmly now, then closed her eyes again and let out one last sigh, like a sigh of relief. As if the malign force that had made her tremble had been sucked out of her at the touch of my hand. The sound of my voice.

I had caught her as she fell. I had saved her. I was the catcher in the rye.

If a body catch a body coming through the rye . . .

The line hung there in my head, like a magic formula. I had a hunch as to what had probably happened: the girl had confused me with her father and that had driven away the monsters. Natsu and I looked at each other, and I realized that she was thinking the same thing. I also realized, very clearly and very insistently, that I had rarely in my life had such a feeling of perfect intimacy.

We stayed there, in silence, for a few more minutes, just to be on the safe side. The girl was sleeping now, her face calm, her breathing regular.

Natsu put the pillow back in place and tucked her in. We didn't talk until we were back in the kitchen.

"I told her her father had to go away on a business trip. A very long trip, abroad, and I didn't know when he'd be back. I don't know how, but she knew everything. Maybe she heard me talking on the phone to someone when I thought she was asleep. I don't know. But one evening we were watching television and there was this scene in a film where policemen followed a robber and arrested him. Without looking at me, Midori asked me if that was how they'd arrested her daddy."

She broke off. Clearly she didn't like to tell – or remember – that story. She poured herself another rum. Then she realized she hadn't asked me if I wanted one. I did, and poured one for myself.

"Obviously I asked her what she was thinking of. Her daddy was away on business, I said. She didn't believe me, she replied, but that was the last time she asked about it. Since then, maybe two or three nights a week, she's been having nightmares. The terrible thing about it is that she almost never wakes up. If she woke up I could talk to her, reassure her. But she doesn't. It's as if she's a prisoner in a strange, frightening world. And I can't enter it, I can't save her."

I asked her if she had taken Midori to see a child psychologist. A stupid question, I thought, as soon as I'd asked it. Of course she'd taken her to a psychologist.

"We go once a week. Gradually we've managed to get her to tell us her dreams . . ."

"Does she dream that they're coming to get you, too?"

Natsu looked at me in surprise for a few moments. What did I know about what goes on in the head of a six-year-old girl? She nodded weakly.

"The psychologist says it's going to take a long time. He says it was a mistake not telling her the truth from the start. He says we should be able to tell her eventually that her father is in prison. Unless her father is released before that. We decided to wait for the result of the appeal before making a decision about exactly how and when."

When she said *the result of the appeal* I felt a hollow stab in the pit of my stomach.

"It isn't going to be easy. You do realize that, I hope?"

She nodded.

I remembered my own childhood nightmares. I remembered nights spent with the light on, waiting to see the daylight filter through the shutters before I could finally sleep. I remembered other nights when the fear was so unbearable that I spent all night sleeping on a chair outside my parents' bedroom, wrapped in a blanket. I was eight or nine. I knew perfectly well that I couldn't ask to sleep in their bed, because I was too old. So, when the nightmares woke me, I would get up, take the blanket, drag a chair from the living room all the way to the door of my parents' bedroom, would curl up on it, cover myself and stay there until dawn, when I would go back to my own little room.

The anguish of those nights came back to me, and I felt the same painful, helpless compassion for the child I was then and that beautiful, unhappy little girl now.

I didn't say all this to Natsu. I'd have liked to, I think, but I couldn't.

Instead, I stood up. It had got very late, I said. I'd better go, because apart from anything else I was working the next day. We walked out into the hall.

"Wait a moment," she said.

She went back into the kitchen, and came back again a few seconds later with a CD.

"It's the one we were listening to tonight. Take it."

I held it in my hand, looking at the title, silently, trying to think of something to say. In the end, though, I just said goodnight and slipped out, as quick as a thief, and down the stairs of that quiet apartment block. Ten minutes later I was in my car, listening to the CD as I drove home along the cold, deserted street.

Home was cold and deserted, too.

15

Tancredi's call came as I was leaving the clerk of the court's office, after a depressing look through a number of files.

"Carmelo."

"Where are you, Guerrieri?"

"In Tahiti, on holiday. Didn't I tell you?"

"Be careful. With jokes like that, someone might die laughing."

He told me he had to see me. From his tone it was clear it was about something he had no intention of telling me over the phone, so I didn't ask him any questions. He suggested we meet in a bar near the courthouse, and twenty minutes later we were sitting in front of two of the worst cappuccinos in the region.

"Do you have the passenger list?"

Tancredi nodded. Then he looked around, as if to check that no one was watching us. No one could have been watching us, because the bar was empty, apart from the fat lady behind the counter. The perpetrator of those delightful cappuccinos.

"Among the passengers coming from Montenegro was a gentleman who's quite well known in certain circles."

"How do you mean?"

"Luca Romanazzi, class of 1968. He's from Bari, but lives in Rome. Twice arrested and tried for Mafia connections and drug trafficking, twice acquitted. Middle-class family, father a municipal employee, mother a nursery school teacher. Brothers normal. A normal family. He's the proverbial black sheep. We're sure he took part in a series of armoured-car robberies – according to various informants – and that he was involved in trafficking with Albania. Drugs and luxury cars. But we have nothing that'll stick. The son of a bitch is good."

"He could have organized this whole operation."

"Yes, he could. He could also be an accomplice of your client's, to take another plausible hypothesis."

"I need to show his face to Paolicelli."

"Of course."

"That means I need a photo, Carmelo."

He didn't reply. He looked around again, moving only his eyes, and then took a yellow envelope from the inside pocket of his jacket and gave it to me.

"I'd be grateful if this stayed confidential, Guerrieri. And after you've shown it to your client I'd be grateful if you burned it, or ate it, or whatever you like."

I was listening to him with the envelope in my hand.

"And I'd also be grateful if you put it away. For example, doing a complicated thing like putting it in your pocket before everyone in the bar realizes that Inspector Tancredi delivers supposedly confidential papers to a criminal lawyer."

I didn't bother saying that "everyone in the bar" seemed to me a bit of an exaggeration, seeing that the lady behind the bar had been joined only by a little old man who was drinking a double brandy, completely uninterested in us or the rest of the world. I thanked him and put the envelope in my pocket. Tancredi was already getting up to go back to police headquarters.

16

Every job has its breaking points, its fault lines. Cracks on the wall of consciousness that make you realize – or should make you realize – that you ought to stop, change, do something else. If it's at all possible. Of course it almost never is. And besides, you almost never have the courage to even think about it.

I had many symptoms of a breaking point coming. One of them was the nausea I always felt when I had to visit the prison. It would begin as a creeping anxiety when I was still in my office, continue as I was on my way there, and turn to disgust when I was at the checkpoint and they were registering my name, taking my mobile phone, locking it in a cabinet, and opening the first of the many doors I would have to go through to get to the interview room.

That day the disgust was particularly strong, and physical.

As I waited for them to bring in Paolicelli, I asked myself what I would do if he recognized the man in the photo. I'd go back to Tancredi, and he would tell me that he couldn't do anything else for me. Taking a photo from the Flying Squad databank was already a big favour. He could hardly start an investigation, based purely on the hypothesis that Luca Romanazzi had stuffed Fabio Paolicelli's car full of drugs, either directly or through an intermediary. I didn't need a policeman or a private detective for an investigation like this, I needed a magician.

If Paolicelli didn't recognize the photo, it was all a lot simpler. I had done my best – nobody could deny that – and all I could do now was limit the damage. My duty became much simpler. The appeal was completely hopeless and we had to plea-bargain. No dilemma – I'd had enough of dilemmas, even more so in this case than in others – no effort, nothing to study. Nothing.

And into these reflections there crept, like some quick-moving, repulsive little animal creeping into the well-scrubbed kitchen of a house in the country, the idea that if things went that way, Paolicelli would be in prison for quite a long time.

And I'd know how to make use of that time.

"What is it?" he asked me as I held out the photo.

"Take a look at it and tell me if you know this man or if you've ever seen him."

He looked at it for a long time, but, from the way he started to shake his head imperceptibly, I realized that my investigation was already over. The shaking became more marked and at last he looked up at me and gave me back the photo.

"Never seen him. Or if I have, I've forgotten. Who is he?"

I was tempted to reply that, since he didn't know him, it didn't matter. But I didn't do that.

"He's a criminal. A top-level drug trafficker. At least the police suspect he is, though they've never been able to pin anything on him. He was on board the same ferry as you. My suspicion was that he had something to do with what happened to you."

"What do you mean, your suspicion *was*? Don't you still suspect him?"

It was an intelligent question, and I gave a stupid answer.

"You didn't recognize him."

"What does that mean? I didn't see who put the drugs in my car. How could I recognize him? If there's a reason to suspect this character had something to do with my case, what difference does it make if I don't recognize him?"

His reply annoyed me. I had to make an effort to restrain the impulse to give him a curt answer, to the effect that I was the lawyer and he was the client. I was the professional and he was the prisoner. I had to make an effort not to pay him back for the fact that he was right.

"Theoretically, it shouldn't make any difference. But in practice, even though we may suspect this man, we have no pretext to present this suspicion in court if you don't recognize him. If you can't say that you noticed this man hanging around your car, for example. Or that he was unusually interested in you, in when you'd be going back —"

I broke off abruptly, realizing that what I was saying could be taken as a suggestion. I could be telling him that *if* he said these things, whether they were true or not, there was a glimmer of hope. It could be construed as an incitement to invent a false story, to pretend that he recognized him.

"In other words, you didn't see him, you don't know him, and I can't stand up in front of the appeal court judges and say, please acquit Signor Paolicelli because a man suspected by the police of being a criminal, a trafficker, was travelling on the same ferry."

"And what difference would it make if I recognized him?"

I shook my head. He was right again. It didn't make a damned bit of difference. I was starting to realize how stupid, amateurish and childish I had been to embark on an investigation like this without knowing in which direction

I was going. An old marshal in the *carabinieri* once told me that the secret of success in an investigation lies in knowing what the real objective is. If you go into it blindly, you don't achieve anything and may even make things worse.

I felt very tired. "I don't know. It was worth a try. If you'd recognized the man it might have given me something to work on. I don't even know how we could have worked on it, but this way I don't see any prospects."

"Show the photo to my wife. Maybe she noticed some detail that escaped me."

Right, once again. In theory.

I would show the photo to Natsu but, for some reason, I was certain she wouldn't recognize him. I was certain this whole thing would come to nothing and that Paolicelli would come to a bad end.

I saw all this clearly, and felt like someone watching from a safe vantage point as someone else drowns. Like someone pretending, even to himself, that he's saddened by what's happening.

But it isn't true. Because in fact he's pleased. Disgustingly pleased.

As I left the prison, I told myself that sooner or later I'd have to find myself an honest job.

17

Natsu came into the office the next day and, as I'd expected, didn't recognize the man in the photo. She took it, asked me who he was, and looked at it carefully, for a long time. Such a long time that after a while I thought that, against all expectation, she had recognized him. Then, just as I was thinking this, she gave me back the photo, pursing her lips and shaking her head.

We were both silent. She seemed to be looking for something, at some indeterminate point above her and to her left. Then her eyes changed direction completely, moving down and to her right. It seemed as if she was having a dialogue with herself. She wasn't paying any attention to me, which gave me a chance to look at her for a long time, savouring her features, her hazel eyes. And vaguely thinking many things. Too many things.

"There's nothing we can do, is there?" She said this with a strange intonation in her voice. Hard to say if it was resignation, calm despair or something else. Like an unwitting hint of anticipation.

I shrugged and shook my head. "I don't know. This was worth a try. I can't think of anything else that makes sense."

"So what do we do?"

"We wait for the appeal hearing, hoping we get a bright idea, or that something happens."

"It won't."

"If nothing new happens, the only sensible thing to do is to plea-bargain. As I told you. As I already told him."

"In other words, he gets a reduction in his sentence and stays in prison."

"Theoretically, after the plea-bargaining we could try asking for house arrest. However . . ."

I left the sentence hanging. It didn't take me long to realize why. The idea of him coming home, even if he was under house arrest, was unbearable, unthinkable.

"However?" Her question wedged itself into my thoughts and my shame.

"Nothing. A technical matter. After the plea-bargaining we can try asking for house arrest. I wouldn't hold out too much hope, because such a large quantity of drugs was involved. But we can try."

"And if they don't give him house arrest, how long will he have to stay inside?"

Once again I had the same strange feeling I'd had before. The feeling I didn't quite understand the real reason for the question. Did she want to know how long she would be separated from her husband, or did she want to know how much time she had at her disposal?

How much time *we* had at our disposal.

Was she really asking that or was I projecting it onto her?

Because I was certainly wondering it myself. I can see that clearly now: at the time I was aware of it in a vague kind of way – although clearly enough to feel a mixture of shame and longing.

Longing for her – Natsu – and for the child. For the family I didn't have. The family of a man who was in prison, a man I should be protecting and defending.

The longing of a thief.

"It's hard to say right now. Even after the sentence has been made final, it's still possible for there to be some reduction, time off for good behaviour, day release. It depends on a lot of factors."

I paused.

"Certainly it'll be a few years, even with the most optimistic forecast."

She didn't say anything. I couldn't figure out the expression on her face. I was searching for the words to say that we could see each other again. Outside the office. Like last night. Go for a drive, listen to a little music, talk. Other things.

The longing of a thief.

I couldn't find the words. My hypocritical phrase about the most optimistic forecast was the end of the conversation, and of our encounter.

When Natsu left, I told Maria Teresa that I didn't want to answer the phone for half an hour, let alone see any clients who dropped by, as sometimes happened, without having an appointment.

Then I went back to my chair and took my head in my hands. The situation was out of my control, I told myself.

18

By the time I closed the office, Maria Teresa had been gone for a while.

I got home, took some ice cream from the fridge, ate it, spent half an hour with the punchball, did push-ups until my arms were numb, then got into the shower.

I wondered where Margherita was at that moment, what she was doing, but I couldn't imagine it. I probably didn't want to.

I dressed and went out. Alone and without an aim, as was happening more and more often.

I had the impulse to call Natsu and ask her if she wanted me to drop by and see her.

I didn't do it. Instead I walked around the windswept city.

Something strange and unpleasant was stirring inside. Maybe what had happened when Sara left me was about to happen again: insomnia, depression, panic attacks. The idea was a worrying one, but no sooner had I thought it than I realized it wouldn't happen.

I was a permanent misfit now. I had secured a stable, mediocre unhappiness for myself, I thought. I'd insured myself against overwhelming unhappiness by settling for a permanent feeling of dissatisfaction and unmentionable desires. Then I thought, no, these were banal, pathetic musings, I was just feeling sorry for myself. I've always hated people who feel sorry for themselves.

So I decided to go and buy some books.

At that hour – it was eleven – I would find only one place open where I could buy books and also chat. The Osteria del Caffellatte, which in spite of its name is a bookshop.

It opens at ten o'clock at night and closes at six in the morning. The owner, Ottavio, is a former schoolteacher who suffers from chronic insomnia. He hated his work as a teacher all the years he was forced to do it. Then an old aunt, who didn't have any children or any other relatives, left him some money and a small building right in the centre of town. A ground floor and two apartments on the upper floors, one on top of the other. It was the opportunity of a lifetime, and he jumped at it. He moved into the second-floor apartment and converted the ground floor and first floor into a bookshop. As he couldn't sleep at night, he came up with those unusual opening hours. Many people said it was a ridiculous idea, and yet it worked.

There are always people in the Osteria del Caffellatte. Not many, it's true, but there are people there all the time. Obviously, there are some strange characters among them, but most are normal people. Who must be the strangest of all, if they're out buying books at four o'clock in the morning.

There are three small tables and a small bar counter, if you want to drink something or eat a slice of one of the cakes Ottavio makes in the afternoon before he opens. Early in the morning you can have breakfast with the same cakes and a caffè latte. If you're in the shop when it closes, he offers you any left-over cake, says see you tomorrow, closes the shop, and then stands in front of the entrance and smokes his only cigarette of the day. Then he goes for a walk around the awakening city, and just as other people are starting work he returns home and goes to sleep, which is something he can only do by day.

Inside the bookshop, there were three girls sharing a joke. Every now and again they looked in my direction and laughed louder. So, I thought. My trajectory is over. I'm a ridiculous man. Or more likely, I'm just terminally paranoid.

Ottavio was sitting at one of the little tables in the tiny bar area, reading. When he saw me come in, he waved and then went back to his reading. I started walking around between the counters and the shelves.

I picked up a copy of Musil's *The Man without Qualities*, leafed through it, read a few pages, and put it back. I've been doing that for some years. Forever, in fact. With Musil, and above all with Joyce's *Ulysses*.

Every time, I'm confronted with my own ignorance and I tell myself I ought to read these books. But I never even get as far as buying them.

I don't suppose I'll ever know first-hand the adventures – if that's the right word – of Stephen Dedalus, Leopold Bloom or Ulrich. I've resigned myself to that, but whenever I'm in a bookshop, I still leaf through those volumes, as a kind of ritual of imperfection. My own.

After a little more wandering, I was attracted by a beautiful cover with a very beautiful title. *Nights in the Gardens of Brooklyn*. I'd never heard of the author – Harvey Swados – or the publisher – Bookever. I read a few lines of the introduction by Grace Paley, was won over, and decided I'd get it.

A young policeman came in. He went up to Ottavio and asked him something. There was a police car double-parked outside.

I spotted a book called *Nothing Happens by Chance*. I decided it referred to my case – whatever my case was – and I'd get that one, too. The policeman went out with a book in a small bag. It's a kind of bag you only find in Ottavio's shop. On one side there's a drawing of a steaming cup of caffè latte, a blue cup without handles, and the name of the shop. On the other side, printed on the plastic, a page of a novel, a poem, a quotation from a sage. Things that Ottavio likes and wants to pass on to his nocturnal customers.

I already felt much better. For me, bookshops are a tranquillizer and an antidepressant. The girls had left without my noticing. Now Ottavio and I were alone. I went up to him.

"Hi, Guido. How's it going?"

"Fine. What did the policeman buy?"

"You wouldn't believe me if I told you."

"Try me."

"*Uninterrupted Poetry*."

I was surprised. "Paul Eluard?"

"Yes. You must be one of the three or four lawyers in the world who know that book. And he must be the only policeman."

"He won't get far."

"I agree. What are you getting?"

I showed him the books I'd chosen and he approved. Especially the Swados.

"And what are you reading?"

He was holding a small book with a cream-coloured cover, from another publisher I didn't know: Botanical Editions.

He handed it to me. The title was *The Manumission of Words*. There was a subtitle, *Notes for a Seminar on Writing*. No author's name on the cover.

I leafed through it and read a few paragraphs.

Our words are often devoid of meaning. This happens because we have worn them out, exhausted them, emptied them through excessive and above all unwitting use. We have turned them into empty shells. In order to tell stories, we must regenerate our words. We must give them back their meaning, texture, colour, sound, smell. And to do this we have to break them into pieces and then rebuild them.

In our seminars we give this process of breaking and rebuilding the name "manumission". The word manumission has two meanings, apparently very different. The first meaning is synonymous with tampering, violating, causing damage. The second, which derives directly from ancient Roman law (manumission was the ceremony at which a slave became a free man), is synonymous with liberation, redemption, emancipation.

The manumission of words encompasses both these meanings. We take words to pieces (we manumit them, in the sense of tampering with them, violating them) and then we put them back together (we manumit them, in the sense of liberating them from the bonds of verbal conventions and meaningless phrases).

Only after manumission can we use our words to tell stories.

"Is this your only copy?"

"Yes, but you can have it, if you like. Why are you interested in it?"

Yes, why was I interested in it?

I have an old wish that I recently expressed, and a friend has assured me it'll come true. The wish is to become a writer, and seeing this book I thought I'd do a bit of studying. Just to make things easier for the department responsible for magic lamps, four-leaf clovers and falling stars.

I fantasized a little about these paragraphs and about other things. Without replying to Ottavio's question. He respected my silence, and didn't speak until he was sure I'd come back down to earth.

"You're not crazy about your work, are you?"

I gave a kind of sneer. It was true, I wasn't crazy about my work.

"And if you could change professions, what would you do?"

This is getting to be an epidemic. Everyone's asking me about my wishes. Come on, out with it, you've been ganging up on me behind my back.

"I'd like to be a writer. I like books more than anything else. I like reading them and I'd like to write them, if I can. Of course, I don't really know if I can, seeing as I've never had the courage to try."

Ottavio simply nodded and said nothing. I like people who don't make stupid comments. And sometimes the best way not to make stupid comments is not to say anything at all.

"How about a drink?"

"Sure."

"Rum?"

"Rum would be fine."

He took a bottle from the bar counter and poured two doubles. We drank and chatted for a while about a whole lot of things. From time to time people came in. Some bought books, some just browsed.

A man of about fifty, in a jacket, tie and coat, slipped into his trousers a copy of *The Trilogy of the City of K.*, buttoned up his coat and headed for the exit. Ottavio noticed, asked me to excuse him for a moment, and caught up with the man at the door.

He said he would like to be able to give books away. But unfortunately he couldn't. He was obliged to make people pay for them. He said this without a hint of sarcasm. The man stammered a few words, something to the effect that he really didn't know what he, Ottavio, was talking about. Patiently, like someone who's said the same thing many times, Ottavio told him there were two options. Either the man paid for the book and took it away – he could even have a discount – or else he could put it back on the shelf, go home to bed as if nothing had happened, and come back whenever he liked. The man said all right then, he'd buy it. And in an extraordinary, surreal sequence he went to the cash desk, pulled the book out of his pants, paid – getting the discount – took his nice little bag, bade everyone goodnight, and left.

"Some people are completely shameless," I said.

"You have no idea. But somehow I can't get angry with people who try to steal books. I've stolen so many myself. How about you?"

I said I'd never stolen a book. Not physically stolen. I'd read lots in bookshops, without buying them. Not in his shop, I hastened to add.

Then I looked at my watch and realized how late it was. I had to be in court the next day. I asked him how much I owed him.

"The drinks are on the house. The books you have to pay for, because, as I told that man, I'm really not able to give them away."

19

I had only just got in to the office when Maria Teresa put through a call from Colaianni.

He didn't beat about the bush. He had to talk to me, he said, but he'd rather do it face to face.

Usually after a sentence like that, I would have made a joke about magistrates always thinking their phones were tapped, but something in his voice stopped me. So I simply asked how we could talk face to face, seeing that he was in Rome and I was in Bari. He said he was going to be in Foggia in two days' time, to visit someone in the prison there. If I could get there after he'd finished, we could meet, have a bite together and talk. OK, the day after tomorrow. Bye, see you then.

After putting the phone down I felt strangely euphoric. After so many years of being a defence lawyer, for the first time I had a sense of what detectives feel when an investigation produces results. Because there was no doubt about it. Colaianni had some information about the lawyer Macrì. Some important information.

My first impulse was to call Natsu.

Hi, Natsu, I wanted to tell you there's news. What news? Well, to tell the truth I don't know, but I'll know the day after tomorrow in Foggia. Oh, by the way, what are you doing tonight?

My mental ramblings were fortunately interrupted by Maria Teresa, who put her head in through the door and told me Signora Pappalepore and her daughter had arrived. New clients. They had phoned the day before and had made an appointment. I told her to send them in, but as soon as they crossed the threshold a neon sign saying "Watch out" started flashing frantically in my head.

The younger of the two women was about fifty, all dolled up as if she was still a girl, with ridiculous red glasses, Seventies-style clothes, bright red lipstick and yellow hair. The other one was an elderly lady, wearing the same lipstick and glasses as thick as the bottoms of Coca-Cola bottles.

I asked them to take a seat. The younger one helped the elderly one to sit down, then sat down herself and gave me a somewhat disquieting smile.

"How can I help you?" I said, smiling affably and a bit stupidly.

"Who is this young man?" the old woman said as if I wasn't there, looking at her daughter.

"He's the lawyer, mother. You remember we came about the lawsuit?"

"Is he Raffaele's cousin?"

"No, mother, Raffaele's cousin died ten years ago."

"Oh . . ." She seemed to calm down. A few moments of silence followed and I started to get worried.

"So . . ." I prompted them, smiling as stupidly as before.

"Avvocato Guerrini, we have to bring a lawsuit. Something serious is going on."

I was going to point out that my name was Guerrieri, not Guerrini, but decided there was no point.

"There's a conspiracy against us in our apartment building."

Oh, great, I'm crazy about conspiracies. These two mad-women were all I needed right now.

"Who is this young man?" the old woman said, looking into empty space now.

"Avvocato Guerrini, mother. For the lawsuit, don't you remember?"

"Is he married?"

"I don't know, mother. That's his business. Do you want a sweet?"

The old lady said yes and the younger one took a bag from a pastry-shop out of her handbag. She took out a red sweet, unwrapped it and put it in her mother's mouth. Then she asked me if I wanted one. I smiled again, through pursed lips, and said no, thanks.

"Some very serious things are happening, Avvocato Guerrini. The people in our building have got together to destroy us. It's like a kind of . . . what do you lawyers call it?"

Yes, what did we lawyers call it?

". . . a Mafia-style organization."

A Mafia-style organization. Of course. Why didn't I think of that?

"They attack us every day and now we've decided to bring a lawsuit against them."

"But is this young man Marietta's son?"

"No, mother, Marietta's son lives in Busto Arsizio. This is the lawyer."

"Whose son is he?"

"I don't know, mother. He's the lawyer, we've come about the lawsuit."

At this point, the old lady suddenly decided to address me directly. "Young man, are you Signora Marzulli's nephew?"

"No, signora," I replied politely.

"This is the lawyer. Signora Marzulli's nephew is a male nurse."

"A lawyer. And so young. But he must be Raffaele's . . ."

Cousin? No, signora, I'm not Marietta's son, who seems to be living in Busto Arsizio, I'm not Signora Marzulli's nephew, a male nurse apparently, and I'm not even Raffaele's cousin, who for all I know may have been a lawyer although he's dead now. I'd also like to get rid of you and do a bit of work, but I realize that's an unlikely prospect.

I didn't say that. In fact I didn't say anything, because I noticed that the old lady had started to sway slowly to her left, leaning on the arm of the chair. For a moment, I had the impression she was falling. Maybe she was having a heart attack or something. I imagined all the logistical problems that would arise, getting the body removed. This wasn't my lucky afternoon, I told myself.

But the woman wasn't dying. After swaying for about thirty seconds, almost hypnotically, she straightened her skirt and became still again.

In the meantime, her daughter had continued telling me about the Mafia-style organization that had taken over their apartment building in the Via Pasubio.

This criminal gang had been intimidating them through such things as hanging out their washing contrary to housing regulations and illegal possession of stereo units, not to mention what Signor Fumarulo the surveyor got up to. Fumarulo lived alone and was always bringing women home with him, even in the evening. Once, meeting him in the lift, she had told him that he ought to stop doing it. He had told her not to be such a pain in the arse – as if it was all her fault. She had retorted that he should be careful about what he said, and that she would sue him along with all the others.

"And so Mother and I thought of suing everyone in the building. And then" – she leaned slightly towards me across the desk, conspiratorially – "the money we're awarded in damages we'll share with you, Avvocato, fifty-fifty."

My brain was working frantically to find a way out. Without finding it.

In the meantime the old lady had woken up. "Are you the dentist?"

"No, signora, I'm not the dentist."

". . . Because I have an abscess, just here . . ." and she opened her mouth and stuck a finger inside, so that I could get a good look at the abscess, and everything else.

"He isn't the dentist, mother. He's the lawyer. Do you want another sweet?"

This lasted for at least half an hour, during which the old woman asked me another four or five times if I was Marietta's son or Signora Marzulli's nephew. And especially if I was married.

Whenever she asked me this last question, she would wink cunningly at her daughter.

Finally I had a stroke of genius.

I would be happy to take on their case, I said. And of course, what was happening in their building was a scandal. Something would have to be done as soon as possible, and I would do it. There was just one small formality to be got through first. To bring a lawsuit, you had to pay an advance of – I tried to think of a really off-putting figure – let's say five thousand euros. Unfortunately that was the law, I lied. So I asked the younger Signora Pappalepore to pay me five thousand before I could proceed. Cash was best, though a cheque would be fine too. But I had to have it at once.

She became evasive. Obviously she didn't have that much cash on her, and unfortunately she'd left her chequebook at home. I told her she had to bring it in as soon as possible, tomorrow, or the day after tomorrow at the latest. As I said this, I tried as best I could to look like the worst kind of money-grubbing crook. The kind of person you'd want to get away from as quickly as possible, and never approach again.

"Shall we make an appointment for tomorrow?" I said, with a greedy expression on my face.

"I'll phone you tomorrow, or the day after tomorrow." She was worried now. She'd ended up in the hands of an unscrupulous opportunist and wanted to get out of here as quickly as she could.

"All right, but please, no later than the day after tomorrow."

Of course, she assured me, no later than the day after tomorrow. And now I really must excuse her, but she had to go, because it was time to change her mother's incontinence pad.

In that case, I wouldn't keep her any longer. Good evening. Good evening to you too, signora.

And no, I'm not Marietta's son, not even Signora Marzulli's nephew.

And thank God, I'm not the dentist.

20

It was very cold in Foggia that morning, so it felt good to enter the restaurant, which was not only warm but full of wonderful smells. Colaianni was already there, sitting at a table with two disreputable-looking individuals: his police escort.

We hugged, and exchanged the kind of small talk you'd expect from men of a certain age who'd been students together. The two policemen stood up without a word and went and sat down at another table, close to the entrance.

"How many years have you been in Rome now?"

"Too many. And I'm getting really pissed off. Especially with working in the anti-Mafia field. We keep arresting traffickers and dealers, we spend hundreds of thousands of euros on phone taps, we constantly interview people who've turned State's evidence, or are pretending to, and absolutely nothing changes. I ought to find myself an honest job."

Right, I thought. Exactly the same thing I had said to myself a few days earlier, leaving the prison. Here we were, the finest examples of a generation at the height of its professional success.

I didn't say any of this and he continued. His tone wasn't jokey any more, it had turned bitter, in a way I would never have expected from Andrea Colaianni.

Unlike me, he had always been passionate about his work, had really believed in it. He had thought that working out of a Prosecutor's Department, you could change the world. But life is a little more complicated than that.

"I'm increasingly uncomfortable with this job. Do you remember how I was just after the examination?"

I remembered it very well. At the time he had passed his public examination, we saw each other every day. At twenty-five he had already achieved his main aim in life. To be a magistrate. Whereas I was still young and footloose and would stay that way for a while longer.

"I couldn't wait to start. I couldn't wait to be a prosecutor. I was ready to change things. To bring about justice." He looked me in the eyes. "Big words, eh?"

"How does that song go? The one by De Gregori? *You were looking for justice and you found the law.*"

"Exactly. When I started I felt like an avenging angel. Now – would you believe this? – I feel sick every time I have to arrest someone. A few days ago, in the corridors of the courthouse, I ran into a prisoner in handcuffs being led by a guard. He was a man of about sixty, who looked like a stationer, a grocer, whatever. I've seen hundreds of people in handcuffs. All kinds of people. Scared, arrogant, dazed, indifferent. All kinds, and I should be used to it. It shouldn't have any effect on me. The guard was walking ahead of him and he was behind. At a certain point he slowed down, or maybe he just couldn't keep up. I don't know. Anyway, the guard gave a jerk on the chain, just like you do when you're walking your dog and it stops too long to sniff something. It was only for a moment, because then the man walked quicker and caught up. I stood there in the corridor watching them walk away. I felt a knot in my stomach. That, too, was only for a moment and then the guys in my police escort asked me if anything was wrong and I walked on. Maybe you understand."

I understood perfectly what he was saying. He made a gesture I had seen many times in the past few weeks. He rubbed his face, hard, as if trying to wipe out something viscous and unpleasant. He didn't manage it. No one ever does.

"If I could, I'd change jobs. Obviously I can't. My destiny is all mapped out. Another few years and I'll be able to ask for a transfer to the office of the Director of Public Prosecutions, where I won't have to do a damn thing. I'll learn to play golf, take a lover – maybe a young secretary? – and happily carry on to the end."

"Hey, hey, hold on. What's happening to you?" It was a stupid question. I knew perfectly well what was happening to him.

"Nothing. A mid-life crisis, I suppose. Have you already had yours? I'm told they pass."

Had I had mine? Yes, I'd had it, and I didn't know if it really had passed. But compared to him I had an advantage. I'd felt out of place my whole life, so I was used to it. For someone with his convictions it must have been very hard.

"Anyway, fuck all that."

At that moment the waiter came up behind me. We ordered buffalo mozzarella, grilled beef, and red wine from Lucera.

"I asked a few of my colleagues about Avvocato Macrì, but no one's ever heard of him. I also asked a few defence lawyers I know, but none of them have heard of him either. In itself that's not particularly strange in a place like Rome. But it's not quite normal either."

No, I thought, it wasn't normal. The world of criminal lawyers and magistrates, even in a big city like Rome, is a small community. Like a village where everyone knows everyone else. If you live in that village and no one has ever heard of you, something's not right. It means you don't work much, or at all. And if that's the case, how do you make a living?

"So I thought I'd do a little research in our databank. It contains documentation on all the anti-Mafia investigations, along with all the court proceedings, over the past ten years, in the whole of Italy. I said to myself: if this Macrì has defended anyone in that kind of trial, I'll find him and then we'll get a better idea of what's going on."

"And did you find him?"

The waiter arrived with the wine and filled the glasses. Colaianni emptied his, in a way I didn't like. Nor did I like the way he refilled it immediately.

He looked me straight in the eyes. "Obviously this conversation never happened."

"I never even came to Foggia."

"Good. I found our Signor Corrado Macrì. But he wasn't in our databank as a defence lawyer. He was there as a defendant, arrested three years ago by an examining magistrate in Reggio Calabria, for associating with the Mafia, drug trafficking and a number of minor charges."

"What did he do?" As I asked the question, it struck me how the roles people play influence the things we say and even the things we think. If Macrì had been my client, I would have asked what he'd been charged with and certainly wouldn't have taken it for granted that he had *done* anything.

Colaianni took a few sheets of paper out of his bag, chose one and started to read the charge sheet.

"Let's see . . . Ah, yes. Corrado Macrì, benefiting from his position as defence counsel of a number of prominent members of the organization – there follows a list – and having been specifically appointed for that purpose, acted as a link between the imprisoned bosses of the organization and those still at liberty. In particular, gaining access, thanks to his position as defence counsel, to various penal institutions

– there follows a list – in which the above-mentioned were confined, he proceeded to inform them of the most significant events that had happened in the organization, agreed with their plans and criminal operations, and proceeded to communicate to those members still at liberty the decisions and orders of the imprisoned bosses."

He stopped – he'd been struggling a bit, and I thought he should have put on his reading glasses – and looked at me.

"He was the go-between," I said.

"Yes. Do you want to know what happened?"

I wanted to know and he told me. Our friend Macrì had been taken into custody on the testimony of two grasses. He had spent several months inside, until one of the grasses changed his story and retracted everything. The case fell apart. Macrì was released on the grounds of insufficient evidence. A few months later he opted for the fast-track procedure and was acquitted.

"And how did he end up in Rome?"

"I don't know. After his acquittal he had his name taken off the register of the Reggio Calabria bar association, and for some reason registered in Rome. Where, as I said, he doesn't seem to put in many appearances in court."

He left the last words hanging in the air and again emptied his glass. He refilled it and then refilled mine.

My brain was working overtime. Macrì was the key to the whole thing, I was sure of it now. One way or another, the drugs found in Paolicelli's car belonged to some of Macrì's clients – or rather, some of his accomplices. When Paolicelli had been arrested, they had sent for the lawyer to keep an eye on what happened, to check what was in the file, to make sure that the investigation didn't lead back to the drugs' real owners.

116

And then there was the matter of the lifting of the sequestration order. The fact that he had gone personally to get it out of the pound. There must have been something still in the car that the customs police had missed, something that had to be disposed of as quickly as possible.

That was if Paolicelli really had nothing to do with it. Because it could also be that Macrì had been sent by the organization to safeguard a member – Paolicelli – who'd had the misfortune to end up in the clutches of the law.

I told my friend what I was thinking and he nodded. He had been thinking the same.

"And now what are you going to do with this information?"

Right. What was I going to do?

I said I would have to think about it. Perhaps, with this as a starting point, I could find out more, maybe by hiring a private detective. The fact was, I hadn't the faintest idea what to do.

When the time came to say goodbye, Colaianni told me he'd really enjoyed seeing me again and talking to me. He said it in a vaguely frightened tone, as if he didn't want me to go. I felt both saddened and embarrassed.

And I wanted to get away. Away from that unexpected fragility, that despair, that sense of defeat.

As I took the ramp to get onto the autostrada I was thinking about my friend Colaianni.

About the things he'd said to me – other than the information about Macrì – and the glimpses of distress that he could barely conceal. I wondered what would have become of his life – of our lives – by the next time we met.

Then the half-deserted autostrada swallowed everything.

21

What did I want to do with this information? Colaianni had asked me.

I didn't know, I'd replied. And it was true, I didn't. I had no idea what I could do with it. I knew now that Macrì was an associate of Mafiosi and drug traffickers. But, when you came down to it, this didn't greatly improve our situation.

I didn't know what to do and that was why I didn't go to see Paolicelli and tell him what I'd found out. If he was innocent I didn't want to arouse any unfounded expectations. And if he was guilty – my doubts had returned with a vengeance, as I'd talked to Colaianni – I didn't want to play the sucker any longer than I had to.

For the same reason, and for others I didn't want to admit even to myself, I didn't call Natsu. Even though I had to restrain the impulse lots of times.

I thought of calling Tancredi, but then I told myself I'd already taken more than enough advantage of our friendship. And besides, I didn't know what to say to him, apart from asking him for advice yet again.

Several days passed in this absurd way.

Then one evening, as I was leaving my office to go home, I heard my name being called. I looked up and saw Natsu in an off-road vehicle. She gave me a shy smile, and made a gesture with her hand, inviting me to join her. I looked round, like someone who has something to hide, crossed the road and got in the car.

Yes, I did have something to hide.

22

"Shall we drive to the sea?"

I said yes. We went along streets that were unusually free of traffic. She drove smoothly, sitting comfortably, deep in her seat, both hands on the wheel, her eyes on the road. For a moment it occurred to me that this was the car in which the drugs had been carried. Then I remembered that the police reports had mentioned a different make and model.

"You're surprised."

It was a statement, not a question. So I didn't reply, just shrugged my shoulders. I let her talk.

"I had a job on for tonight. Then something went wrong and it was called off. But there was no time to warn the babysitter. So when she arrived I decided to go out anyway, and I thought maybe you'd like to go for a drive and a chat."

That evening I wasn't exactly talkative. For the first time she took her eyes off the road – we were outside the city now – to see if I was dead or just asleep.

"Shouldn't I have?"

"You did the right thing. I'm pleased."

She put on a bit of speed. The engine droned, and the car darted forward. She asked me if there was any news for her husband.

I felt a twinge of unease at the question. It was an abrupt reminder of the fact that I was a lawyer and she was the wife of a client of mine who was in prison.

Leaving out a few details – how I'd got hold of the information, and from – I told her what I'd discovered about their former lawyer.

She listened to me in silence until I'd finished. In the meantime we had stopped on a low cliff over towards Torre del Mare. The surface of the water was as black and calm as ink. In the distance the intermittent beam from a lighthouse could be seen.

When Natsu was sure I had nothing else to add, she said, "And now what will you do?"

"I have no idea. In itself the fact that the bastard was arrested – and then acquitted – doesn't get us anywhere. I mean, I don't know how to use this information in court."

"But he put himself forward without either of us contacting him. That must surely mean something."

"Theoretically, yes. In practice, the only thing that's clear from the papers on this case is that you appointed him and your husband confirmed the appointment."

"But they told me —"

"I know, I know. But what do we do? Do I call you to testify at the appeal hearing that a man stopped you in the street and advised you to appoint this lawyer you didn't even know called Macrì, and you followed his advice? Apart from the fact that even if it was true – I mean, even if the judges believed it was true – it wouldn't get us anywhere, the prosecution could simply say that your husband's accomplices told you which lawyer to appoint. And we'd be in the same position as before, maybe even a bit worse off."

I avoided saying that this could be the prosecution's version, or it could be the plain truth. I was sure she'd thought of that herself.

At that precise moment I had an idea. It was a crazy idea,

but with Natsu still silent, I started thinking about it. Yes, I told myself, it might be worth a try, in fact it might be the only thing we could try. Then she interrupted the course of my thoughts. "You know what the worst thing is for me?"

"Not knowing the truth?"

She looked at me in surprise for a few seconds, until she remembered the game of wishes. She searched in her bag, took out a packet of cigarettes, lowered the window and lit one.

She smoked it in silence. Savouring every mouthful and letting the smoke waft away into the surrounding darkness. When she'd finished, she closed the window and shivered, as if only just becoming aware of the cold.

"I'm hungry, but I don't want to be cooped up in a restaurant."

"Uh-huh," I said.

"Of course, like all men who live alone, your larder is full of tins and crap like that."

I told her she shouldn't believe the stereotypes. No, I didn't have a larder full of tins. I had fresh, healthy food in the fridge and if I wanted I could even whip up a quick dinner.

So she said all right, let's go to your place. Ruthlessly suppressing the qualms of my conscience, it struck me that, when you got down to it, there was nothing wrong with the idea. Nothing had to happen. And anyway, it wasn't my fault. I mean, she'd made all the moves. She'd waited for me outside my office, taken me for a drive, suggested coming to my place. It really wasn't my fault. If it had been up to me, nothing would have happened.

A heap of bullshit that stayed with me all the way to my apartment.

*

"What's that?" It was the first thing she said as soon as she stepped inside the door. She was referring to the punchball hanging in the middle of the room which served as both the hall and the living room. A somewhat bizarre thing to have as part of the furnishings, I admit.

"One of my neuroses. Every evening I come home and punch it for half an hour. Look at it this way. It's better than getting drunk, taking drugs or beating the wife and kids. Which I don't have anyway."

"It's nice here. Do you like books or are you just a messy person?"

She was referring to the books piled around the sofa and strewn all over the room. I'd never thought about it, but I told her I liked to have them on the floor because they kept me company.

She spotted the kitchen and headed straight for it.

"Where are you going?"

"I'm looking to see what's in the fridge. I'll make something."

With a certain self-importance, I said I'd already sampled her cooking and now, whether she liked it or not, it was her turn to sample mine. She had accepted the risk when she came to my apartment. If she liked, she could stay with me in the kitchen while I was cooking but it was strictly forbidden for her to touch anything.

There wasn't very much there. I'd exaggerated a bit when I mentioned having lots of fresh food. But I had what I needed to make my speciality. I called it spaghetti *al fumo negli occhi*. Meaning the cook – in this case, me – throws smoke in people's eyes, tries to appear more skilful than he really is.

123

"I'll make pasta. That's the most I can rustle up without advance warning."

Even *with* advance warning, to tell the truth. But I didn't say that.

"Pasta and wine are fine. What are you making?"

"You'll see," I said, and immediately felt ridiculous. Who the hell do you think you are, Guerrieri? This woman is a professional chef, you idiot. Just get on with it and cook the food.

I fried garlic, oil and chillies in a pan. While the spaghetti was boiling I grated some pecorino, chopped some basil, and stoned and sliced a few black olives. I put the pasta, very *al dente*, into the frying pan and added the pecorino and the rest.

Natsu said she liked watching me cooking, which made me tingle all over. A nice but dangerous sensation. I didn't reply, quickly laid the table, told her to sit down, and carried over the brimming plates.

We ate, drank and chatted about nothing, with the punch-ball standing guard over us.

When we had finished eating, I put on *Shangri-la* by Mark Knopfler. Then I took my glass and went and sat down on the sofa. She stayed on her chair. When she realized what the disc was, she said she liked 'Postcards from Paraguay' a lot. I put the glass down on the floor, reached for the controls and fast-forwarded to track 10.

She came and sat down next to me, on the sofa, just as the song was starting.

One thing was leading to the next, the voice sang.

Spot on, I thought.

It was the last rational thought I had that night.

23

I didn't have to be in court the next day. I sent Maria Teresa to the courthouse to get some things sorted out at the clerk of the court's office. Not that any of them were urgent, but I needed to be alone.

I had a few things to think over. Quite a few things.

In the first place, I felt like a shit for what had happened last night. It wasn't that I'd been taken by surprise, or that I hadn't had a pretty good idea what might happen. If I'd had a modicum of moral sense, I told myself, I wouldn't have taken Natsu home with me.

I wondered what I would have said if someone had told me a story like that and asked me what I thought. I mean: what I thought about a lawyer who fucked the wife of one of his clients while that client was in prison.

I would have said that lawyer was a piece of shit.

Part of me was looking for excuses for what had happened, and even finding a few. But overall, my inner prosecutor was winning this case hands down. He was so far out in front that I felt like asking him where the hell he'd been last night when I needed him.

I remembered an after-dinner conversation with some colleagues, some years earlier. We'd had a lot to eat and drink. Some of us were little more than boys, others older, people we'd trained with.

I don't know who told the story. It was a true story, he said, which had happened a few years earlier.

There was this guy in prison, accused of murder. An almost hopeless case. He needed a lawyer. A very good one, considering the situation he was in.

But he didn't have the money to pay for a good one. In fact he didn't even have money to pay for a bad one. What he did have was a beautiful wife. One evening she went to see an old, famous and very good lawyer, who was also a notorious womanizer. She told him she wanted him to defend her husband but didn't have the money to pay him. So she suggested payment in kind. He accepted, fucked her – repeatedly, in the office and outside – defended the guy and managed to get him acquitted.

End of story, start of discussion.

"What would you have done?"

Various answers. There were some who thought it hadn't been very good form to do it in the office. Good manners mattered, damn it, whatever the situation. It would have been better to go to a hotel or somewhere else. Others, though, considered that fucking her on the desk was consistent with the nature of the contract they'd entered into. A few timidly expressed ethical qualms, and were howled down.

The young Guerrieri said he would have defended the prisoner for free, without payment in kind, and someone told him he was an idiot and would sing a different tune if something like that ever happened.

Whoever said that was right.

And then I thought of Macrì, and the idea that had come to me the night before. On how I could use the information Colaianni had passed on to me to help Paolicelli out of the mess he was in. Gradually, with my mind going back and forth like a ping-pong ball between these two thoughts – what a shit I was, and what to do with my honourable colleague

Macrì to save my oblivious client Paolicelli – the professional side gained the upper hand.

My idea was to call him as a witness.

It was a crazy idea, because you don't call a lawyer as a witness for the defence. Apart from the fact that there could be an objection on the grounds of lawyer-client confidentiality, calling a lawyer is something that just isn't done, and that's it.

I'd never actually seen it done. I didn't even know if having previously been the defendant's counsel constituted a formal impediment to being a witness – what they called a conflict of interest.

So first of all I took a look at the code. It turned out there was no *a priori* conflict of interest. It could be done, theoretically anyway.

It was the kind of situation in which you really need a second opinion. Not for the first time, I realized I didn't have a single colleague I could turn to. I didn't trust many of them, and none of them were really my friends. For something like this, I needed a friend who knew what he was talking about. And could keep his mouth shut.

I could only think of two people. Curiously, both were prosecutors. Colaianni and Alessandra Mantovani.

I didn't really want to call Colaianni again, but it struck me that this was a good opportunity to talk to Alessandra again after all this time. I hadn't seen or heard from her since she'd left Bari to work in the Prosecutor's Department in Palermo. She'd been escaping from something, like many people. Only she had done it more decisively than most.

She answered after a lot of rings, just when I was about ready to hang up. We exchanged a few jokes, the kind you tell to re-establish contact, to revive the old familiarity.

"It's nice to hear from you, Guerrieri. I sometimes think you and I should have got together. Things might have gone better for me. Instead, the only men I meet are losers, which starts to be a bit of problem when you're already forty."

I am a loser. I'm a bigger loser than any of the men you go out with. I'm also an idiot and if you knew what I did last night you'd agree with me.

I didn't say that. I said we still had time, if she really liked lawyers with a dubious past and an uncertain future. I'd go to Palermo, she could dismiss her police escort, and we'd see how it worked out.

She laughed. Then she repeated that it was nice to hear from me, and maybe it was time to tell her the reason I was calling. I told her. She listened carefully, stopping me only to ask if I could clarify a few points. When I'd finished, I asked her what she thought of my idea.

"It's true that in theory a defence counsel's testimony is admissible. In practice, I very much doubt they'll allow you to call him unless you can give them a good reason – a *very* good reason – to do so. And your suspicions aren't a very good reason."

"I know, that's my problem in a nutshell. I need to find a way to get that testimony admitted."

"You need to put the defendant on the stand first, and his wife. Let them tell the story of how this lawyer came to be involved. Then you can try, though I wouldn't bet on the result. Appeal court judges don't like to go to too much trouble."

"Let's suppose they admit the testimony. In your opinion, can he refuse to answer on the grounds of lawyer-client confidentiality?"

She thought for a few moments before replying. "In

128

my opinion, no. Lawyer-client confidentiality is there to safeguard the interests of the client. He could claim it if he thought his testimony would be prejudicial to his former client. When you put it like that . . . I don't know if there are any precedents."

"Of course, I could get my client to state that he releases his former counsel from the obligation to observe lawyer-client confidentiality."

"Yes. That should clinch it. But if I were you I'd read up on this thoroughly and buy a bulletproof vest before I started down this track."

By the time the call was over, I felt better than I had a few minutes earlier, and my idea seemed a lot less ridiculous.

24

In the afternoon I cycled over to the prison. I had to make a real effort, because the idea of seeing Paolicelli, less than a day after what had happened, didn't do much to increase my self-esteem.

But I had to go, because my plan of action was a risky one. And he was the person who'd be taking most of the risks. So I had to explain everything to him, make sure he understood, ask him if he wanted us to try that strategy.

As he entered the interview room, a few scattered images from the previous night suddenly sprang into my head, but fortunately it was only for a moment. When we started talking the images vanished.

I explained to him what the idea was. I told him it was worth a try, but he shouldn't be under any illusions: it was unlikely that the judges would admit Macrì's testimony, and even if they did, it was very unlikely that it would make much difference to the outcome. But in the situation we were in, it was the only alternative to plea-bargaining – although the option of plea-bargaining should be kept open until the day of the hearing.

He made a simple gesture with his hand, as if swatting away a midge or moving a small object. No plea-bargaining, it meant.

I liked that gesture. I liked the dignity of it. I felt an odd kind of solidarity with him.

Maybe it was my way of processing my sense of guilt. I'm going to end up liking the guy, I thought. And that really would be too much.

So I went on explaining to him how we could proceed, how we could try to play the few cards we had in our hands.

"This would be the sequence: first I ask to examine you, then your wife. The judges will allow that, there shouldn't be any problems. You state that you know nothing about the drugs. It's true that you admitted responsibility when you were arrested, but only because you wanted to keep your wife out of it. You suggest a hypothesis on how the cocaine came to be in your car. Then I ask you about your lawyer and you tell us how that relationship started. Your wife tells us the same story, from her point of view."

I looked him in the eyes. He sustained my gaze, with an interrogative undertone in his. What did my look mean? I told him what it meant.

"Obviously this is a dangerous game we'd be playing. We're on a knife-edge. The only way it has any chance of working is if you've told me the whole truth. If you haven't, then both you and I are running very serious risks. In court and especially outside court, remembering the kind of people we're probably dealing with."

"I've told you the truth. The drugs weren't mine. I did some stupid things in the past, but those drugs weren't mine."

What stupid things? The question flashed for a moment in my head and then disappeared, as quickly as it had come, to give way to the same feeling I'd had a little earlier. A liking for him that I didn't want to feel, but which was seeping in like smoke through the cracks in my conscience.

OK. Better to go on.

"I'll have to question you about what you and this lawyer

talked about. In particular, and this is the most important thing, I'll have to ask you if you ever asked him to account for his being there."

"I'm sorry, I don't quite follow."

"I'll ask you this: when you met Avvocato Macrì, either the first time or any of the subsequent times, did you ask him who had suggested him to your wife? Do you understand why I have to ask that?"

"Yes, yes. I do now."

"In fact, while we're at it, answer the question now. That way we can start to memorize it."

He concentrated, touching his chin. The room was silent and I could hear the noise of his fingers rubbing his stubble the wrong way.

"I think it was the second time we met. The first time was just after my arrest, I hadn't seen my wife yet and so she hadn't told me how she'd been advised to appoint him. And anyway I was still in shock, I wasn't thinking clearly. After the custody order was confirmed, I had my first visit from my wife and she told me about the man who'd stopped her in the street. So when Macrì came to visit me again, a few days later, I asked him if he knew who had suggested his name to my wife."

"And what did he say?"

"He said there was no need to worry about that. He said there were people who wanted to take care of me and they would see to everything. He meant his fee. And it was true, we didn't pay anything. A few times I tried to ask him when I had to pay, and how much, and he always told me not to worry."

"Obviously he never told you, or gave you any hint, who these people were?"

"Obviously not."

"All right. Then you'll have to tell me about the other conversations you had with him, especially the one where you quarrelled. I need you to remember as many details as you can. They'll help to make what you say more credible. Keep a notebook in your cell and write down everything you remember. Even if it's something insignificant. All right?"

The interview was over. We called the guards, who took him back to the bowels of the prison. As I walked back through gates and locks and reinforced doors towards the outside world, I was in a contradictory state of mind.

On the one hand, I still felt like a bastard. But we're all good at finding excuses, ways of justifying our actions.

So I told myself, all right, I'd made a mistake, but in the overall balance sheet we were more or less equal. Maybe I was even in credit. I might save this man's life. What other lawyer would have done what I was doing for him?

Getting on my bicycle, I wondered if Natsu would pick me up from my office again, or if she would call me.

Of if I would have the guts to call her.

25

There followed a succession of strange days. Even the texture of them was strange. Packed, and at the same time suspended, as if time had stood still.

Every now and again I would think about Margherita. Sometimes I wondered what she was doing. If she was seeing anyone, if she would ever come back. My thoughts stopped at that point. I never wondered what would happen if she came back. Whenever I thought she was going out with someone I would feel a twinge of jealousy, but it didn't last long. Sometimes, in the evening, I would get the desire to call her, but I never did.

We had talked over the phone during the first months she was away. They had not been long calls and gradually, spontaneously, they had stopped after the Christmas holidays. She had stayed there, over those holidays, and I had thought that must mean something. Congratulations, Guerrieri, good thinking.

I hadn't wanted to think about it any more than that.

Little by little, I had taken all my things out of her apartment. Every time I went there I felt as if I was being watched, and it wasn't a pleasant feeling. So I took what I needed and got out of there as quickly as I could.

In the evening, after work, I'd go to the gym, or else do a bit of training at home. Then I'd have dinner and start reading or listening to music.

I didn't watch television any more. Not that I'd ever watched it much, but now I just didn't put it on at all. I could have sold the TV set and I'd never have noticed the difference.

I would read for a straight two hours, and make notes on what I was reading. I'd started to do it after the night I'd gone to Natsu's apartment and after reading the book on the manumission of words, with the idea that maybe, further down the line, I could try to write. Maybe.

When I finished reading and taking notes I sometimes went to bed, and fell asleep immediately.

At other times – when I felt sure I wouldn't get to sleep – I'd go out for a walk and a drink. I went to places where no one knew me and avoided those I'd been to with Margherita. Like the Magazzini d'Oltremare, where I might meet someone who asked me what I was doing, where I'd been all this time, why Margherita wasn't with me, and so on.

Sometimes I'd meet people and spend a few hours listening to strangers telling their stories. I was in a strange place, an unknown area of my consciousness. A black-and-white film, with a dramatic, melancholy soundtrack, in which 'Boulevard of Broken Dreams' by Green Day stood out. I often listened to that song, and it echoed almost obsessively in my head during my nocturnal walks.

Once, in a little bar in the old city, I met a girl named Lara. She was twenty-five, short, with a pretty, irregular face, and insolent, occasionally restless eyes. She was doing a research doctorate in German literature, she spoke four languages, her boyfriend had just left her, and she was getting drunk, determinedly, methodically, downing straight vodkas one after another. She told me about her boyfriend, herself, her childhood, her mother's death. The atmosphere in the bar was slightly unreal. There weren't many people, the few there were were talking almost in whispers, the stereo was playing Dvořák's *New World* Symphony at low volume, and there was a slight smell of cinnamon in the air, though I had no idea where it was coming from.

After a while, Lara asked me to take her home. I said OK and paid the bill: one vodka for me, five for her. We walked through the city to her place, which was in Madonnella.

Madonnella is a strange neighbourhood. There are beautiful houses there and horrible municipal housing blocks, millionaires' residences and shacks inhabited by pushers and other members of the underclass, all cheek by jowl. In some parts of Madonnella you have the impression you're somewhere else entirely.

In Tangier, for example, or Marseilles, or Casablanca.

Outside her front door, Lara asked me if I wanted to come up. I said no, thanks. Another time, maybe, I added. In another life, I thought. She stood there looking at me for a few moments, surprised, and then burst into tears. She wasn't crying over my polite refusal, obviously. I felt a kind of distant tenderness towards her. I hugged her, and she hugged me and cried louder, sobbing.

"Bye," she said hurriedly, detaching herself from me and going inside. "Goodbye," I said a few seconds later, to the old wooden door and the deserted street.

26

Ever since Margherita had gone away, the hardest day had been Sunday. I'd go out, read, or drive out of the city, and then eat alone in some restaurant where no one knew me. In the afternoon I'd go to the cinema and then wander around Feltrinelli's bookshop. Then back home in the evening to read. At night I'd often wander the streets again, or take another trip to the cinema.

It was on a Sunday morning – a cold, beautiful day, lit by a blinding sun, three days before the start of the appeal hearing – that I finally couldn't help myself and phoned Natsu.

"Guido!"

"Hi. I wanted to —"

"I'm pleased you called me. I'd like to see you."

I've always envied the naturalness of some people – some women mostly – who can openly say what they think and what they want. I've never been able to do that. I've always felt inadequate. Like an intruder at a feast where everyone else knows how to behave.

"So would I. Very much."

There followed a few moments' silence. She was probably thinking, quite rightly, that if I wanted to see her, and had actually called her, I could at least make an effort and suggest something. In the end, she yielded. She must have concluded that I was an incurable case.

"Listen, seeing as it's such a beautiful day, I'm taking Midori to the park. If you like, you could meet us there."

"The Largo Due Giugno park?"

"Yes. See you in half an hour at the little lake, is that OK?"

Fine, in half an hour at the little lake. Bye, see you soon. Bye.

I dressed like someone about to go for a walk in the park on his own. That is, according to my idea of someone about to go for a walk in the park on his own. Jeans, trainers, sweatshirt, worn leather jacket.

I cycled over there and arrived early. I chained my bike to a bicycle rack and went through one of the gates into the park. It was eleven and there were a lot of people. Families, young boys on rollerblades, adults on rollerblades, people jogging and others doing fitness walking. All wearing jumpsuits, expensive shoes and very serious expressions, as if to say, let's be clear about this, we're doing sport, we're not just out for a stroll.

The basketball courts were all full. On a level stretch of grass, a group of girls in kimonos, all black belts in karate, were performing a *kata*. It was a beautiful sight.

I went all round the park three times, to kill time. Then at last I saw Natsu, dressed much the same way I was. Her daughter was near her, in a pink down jacket, puffing away on a bike.

I waved at her and she waved back, cheerfully.

"You remember Guido, Anna?"

I wondered if she remembered that night. Then I realized how stupid that was. She hadn't even woken up. How could she remember anything?

"Hello," she said.

138

"Hello, Anna, how are you?"

"I'm fine. Do you like my bike? Mummy bought it for me and I can already do without the stabilizers."

"You're very good. At your age I didn't even try to take off the stabilizers."

She looked at me closely for a few seconds, to see if I was pulling her leg. Then she must have decided that I did in fact look like the kind of person who would have had difficulties removing the stabilizers from his bicycle.

"And why did you come to the park? Did you bring your children?"

"No, I don't have children."

"Why?"

Because I was too much of a coward to have them, when I had the chance.

"Guido isn't married, sweetheart. When he decides to get married, he'll have children, too."

That's right. Guaranteed.

The girl set off on her bicycle again. Natsu and I walked slowly after her.

We passed a little stand selling ice cream and drinks.

"Mummy, will you buy me an ice cream?"

"Sweetheart, if I buy you an ice cream you won't eat it."

"Please, mummy. A little ice cream. The littlest one they have. Please."

Natsu was about to say something. She looked as if she was giving in. So I asked her if I could buy Midori an ice cream. She shrugged. "Just a little one."

"OK. A little one."

I told the little girl to come with me and she followed me docilely. Natsu didn't come after us.

For a few seconds – the time it took for us to go together

to the little stand, for her to choose the ice cream, and for me to pay for it, take it, and give it to her – I felt an absurd, commonplace, perfect emotion.

I was that little girl's father. We had come here together – the girl, her mother and her father – for a walk in the park. I was buying her an ice cream.

I was going mad, I told myself. And I didn't give a damn. I was happy to be there, happy that *we* were there, and I didn't give a damn.

The little girl took the ice cream and asked me to carry her bicycle for her, and so we resumed walking along the avenues, all three of us. Like a family.

"Anna has a party this afternoon," Natsu said.

"Uh-huh," I said, with the most stolid of my expressions.

"If you don't have anything else to do, I could come and pick you up after I drop her at her friend's house. What do you think?"

What I thought was that the appeal hearing was in three days' time.

I told her I didn't have anything else to do.

27

I visited Paolicelli the day before the hearing. When he came into the interview room I noticed that he looked particularly depressed.

"I've come to go over things with you. Before anything else, we have to decide once and for all what we're going to do. We can still choose to plea-bargain tomorrow morning."

"I'm being stupid, right? I should plea-bargain and limit the damage, shouldn't I? Otherwise the sentence will be upheld, and then God knows when I'll be out of here."

"Not necessarily. But as I've already said many times, if we plea-bargain you can be certain you'll be out in a few years, or at least on day release."

"For weeks I couldn't wait for the hearing to start and I felt really confident. Now I don't know what to do and I'm fucking afraid. What should I do?"

Don't ask me, I can't tell you that. I'm just a professional, I'm here to suggest alternatives, in a detached way, from a technical point of view. I have to present you with the likely outcome of each option. Then the choice has to be yours. I can't take that responsibility.

I didn't say any of that shit. I was silent for just a few seconds, before replying. And when I did reply, neither my voice nor the words I was saying seemed to be coming from me.

"I say: let's go ahead and appeal. If the drugs weren't yours – and I believe they weren't – it isn't right for you to be in prison and we have to get you out. We have to try every possible way. If the drugs were yours, this is the very last moment for you to tell me. I'm not here to judge you. Tell me and tomorrow we'll do the best plea bargain possible."

He looked me in the eyes. I returned his gaze and it seemed to me that his eyes had become watery.

"Let's appeal."

That was all.

I gave him a brief rundown on what would happen the next day and told him his examination would take place during the following hearing. Then I asked him if he had any questions, and fortunately he didn't. So I said goodbye – see you tomorrow in court – and left.

As I left the prison I was about to switch my mobile on again. Then I had second thoughts. Better to avoid any risk, any temptation, at least tonight. For what it was worth.

28

I didn't even feel like the punchball and so, when I got home, I made myself a roll, ate it, and went straight out without bothering to change.

I soon found myself in the streets of the Libertà neighbourhood. Places full of memories of a period of my life, around twenty years ago, when things seemed simpler.

Lost in thought, I stopped in front of the entrance to a kind of private club. From inside came a voice speaking dialect. Seven or eight men were sitting around a table. They were talking loudly, interrupting each other, waving their arms. To the side, two crates of Peroni beer.

They were playing for beer. It was an old game, halfway between a game and a tribal ritual, involving a pack of Neapolitan cards and several bottles of beer. The winner of each round had to drink a bottle of beer.

"Avvocato Guerrieri!"

Tonino Lopez, a fence well known in the Libertà, with a police record as long as your arm. My client for about ten years.

Officially, in the intervals between one arrest and another, he was a greengrocer, and – since for some reason he was particularly fond of me – every two or three months he'd send a crate of fruit to my office, or artichokes, or a jar of olives in brine, or two bottles of rustic wine. Every time, I would phone him at his shop to thank him, and every time, without fail, he would reply in the same way.

"At your service, Avvocato. Always at your service."

Tonino stood up from his folding wooden stool, came up to me and gave me his hand.

"We're playing for beer, Avvocato. Why don't you come in and sit down?"

I didn't even think twice. I said thank you and went in. The air was thick with the smell of alcohol, cigarette smoke and men. Lopez introduced me to the others. I recognized most of them by sight. I'd seen them either on the streets of the neighbourhood or in the corridors of the courthouse. Some said good evening, others nodded. None of them seemed surprised that I was there, in my grey lawyer's suit and tie.

Tonino took another folding stool from where it was propped against the wall, opened it and put it down next to me.

"Take a seat, Avvocato. Have a beer?"

I took a beer and drank half of it in one go. Tonino liked that, I could see it in his face. I had drunk like a man. I thought it would be better to remove my tie. I did so, and looked around.

It was a dirty little room with a single little door of flaking wood, on the side facing the street. The grimy walls were bare apart from two football posters: one showing the Bari team in the good old days, another with Roberto Baggio in a blue shirt, in the middle of a game.

I finished my beer in another two swigs. Tonino opened another and gave it to me. "Do you know how to play for beer, Avvocato?"

I took a long swig of the second beer. I noticed a packet of red Marlboros on the table and had the impulse to take one. I don't know how, and I don't know why, I didn't. To be honest, I've never really known why I quit smoking.

144

I turned to Tonino. "A little. I played it in the army, with guys from Iapigia and San Pasquale."

"So play with us. It's not too late to join in."

A great idea. We were practically in the street. Someone I knew could easily pass and see me, without a tie, surrounded by some of the biggest crooks in the area. Getting drunk on beer, belching and arguing and quarrelling about the strategy of the game. It might end up in a brawl, there'd be knives involved, and with a bit of luck I'd spend the night in a police holding cell. A perfect trajectory.

"Let's play," I replied, feeling a thrill go through me, and thinking, what the hell.

I played with them for a couple of hours, drank a lot of beers, and left when everyone else did. I was drunk, like all the others, and I felt light-headed and free.

When we said goodbye, everyone was very friendly to me. Almost affectionate. It was as if I had got through some kind of initiation ritual with flying colours. A guy with a belly so big it looked fake actually embraced me and kissed me on the cheeks. I felt the rubbery touch of his belly against me. He smelled of beer, cigarette smoke and sweat.

"You're a great guy, Avvocato," he said before turning and staggering away.

I also staggered away and somewhere on the way home I started to sing. I sang old songs from the Seventies. There must be a meaning to everything that was happening to me, I thought.

Fortunately I was too drunk to figure out what it was.

29

I entered the courtroom after a glance at the sheet of paper fixed to the door, with the list of cases that would be heard that morning.

There was the usual menu – petty thefts, building violations, receiving stolen goods – which would be dealt with at the rate of one case a minute, with the presiding judge giving black looks to the defence counsels and even the prosecutor if they dared utter one word more than was strictly necessary. Which was two or three words more than silence.

Mine was apparently the only case where the defendant was in prison, so it should have had precedence. Should have, but in fact they took them as they came.

It was nine-thirty, in other words, the time when the session was supposed to begin. Obviously there was no one there yet. I'd tried to get there on time because I like deserted courtrooms, and sitting there without doing anything helps me to concentrate. I like the sense of anticipation. It's like the way you feel when you leave home early in the morning and there's nobody about yet. When you sit down in a bar near the sea, have your coffee and wait, and the streets gradually fill and you're very aware of everything and you feel as if you're part of something fleeting yet eternal.

Sitting down on the bench in a deserted courtroom gives me a similar feeling. You feel you're part of something. Something important, something pure and ordered.

Not to worry, though. The feeling quickly vanishes – about a quarter to ten, if I have to specify a time – when the courtroom starts to fill up.

"Hey, Guerrieri. What did you do, sleep here?"

See what I mean?

The voice, wavering between a dubious Italian and Bari dialect, belonged to Castellano. I could never remember his first name. His clients were exclusively thieves – all kinds: car thieves, burglars, pickpockets, bag snatchers – and small-time drug dealers. He had been a colleague of mine at university, which didn't mean that we'd been anything remotely resembling friends, since there were more than a thousand students registered on the course.

Short and stocky, with a neck like a bull, almost completely bald apart from the wisps of hair tumbling over his ears. There were more wisps of hair visible above his shirt collar, which was always unbuttoned, just as his tie was always askew.

He wasn't exactly the kind of person you could chat to about Emily Dickinson or the aesthetic question in Thomas Aquinas. Every other word he spoke was "fuck" and during the pauses between cases – and even *while* the cases were being heard – he liked to advertise his erotic fantasies about whichever member of the opposite sex was within his field of vision. He wasn't exactly discriminating: trainees, secretaries, magistrates and defendants could all be the objects of his not very romantic dreams. It didn't matter if they were beautiful or ugly, young or old.

I replied with a vague smile, hoping he would be content with that and praying that he didn't decide to sit next to me and start a conversation. My prayers weren't granted. He put his briefcase down on the bench and sat down, panting.

147

"How's it going, Guerrieri? Everything OK?"

I said yes, thanks, everything was fine. As I said this I rummaged in my briefcase, pretending to be busy. It was a vain attempt: Castellano didn't even notice. He started telling me that he had a case being heard this morning involving two old clients of his who had been given four years each for a series of bag snatches. He asked me if I knew who the judges were going to be. If they were good he'd go ahead with the appeal, if not he would plea-bargain. I told him who the judges were and he thought about it for a moment, then said it wasn't worth taking a risk with them. He would plea-bargain, that way he'd get it over with quickly. And what did I have on for this morning?

Oh, a drug trafficker? How much had he got at his trial? Sixteen years? Fuck, what had he done to get sixteen years? Who the fuck was he, the head of the Medellín cartel? Anyway, who the fuck cares who these bastards are as long as they pay?

Having exhausted the topic of our respective cases, Castellano changed the subject. "Guerrieri, you know I've got a broadband connection in my office now? It's incredible, you can even download films."

I was pretty sure I knew what kind of films Castellano downloaded.

"Yesterday I downloaded this porn movie you wouldn't believe. Then a client came in and while he was talking I was watching the film. With the sound off, obviously."

Then he explained in detail, in case I wasn't a man of the world, the use he made of these films, when there was no one around to piss him off, in the office or at home. And the ideal thing was a laptop, you could even have it with you when you were in bed, I don't know if I'm making myself clear.

I'll be good, I said in my head. If someone or something arrives right now to save me from this pervert, I swear I'll be good. I'll eat my spinach, I won't say bad words, I won't let off stink bombs in the catechism class any more.

This time my wish was granted. His mobile phone rang and he moved away to answer it.

A couple of minutes later – it was now ten – the assistant prosecutor entered the courtroom.

Montaruli. He was good. Before being transferred to the office of the Director of Public Prosecutions, he'd been a front-line assistant prosecutor for many years, responsible for the arrest and conviction of hundreds of common criminals and white-collar thieves. Some of them had been my clients.

It wasn't a job you could do for too long. Everyone has a breaking point, when you realize you've had enough. It had happened to him, too, and so, having passed fifty, he had decided to have an easier life in the office of the Director of Public Prosecutions. An office where – how shall I put this? – no one kills themselves with work.

I stood up to say hello.

"Good morning, Consigliere."

"Good morning, Avvocato. How are you?"

"Very well. It's my client who's in a bit of trouble."

"Which is your case?"

"Paolicelli. The drugs from Montenegro."

The face he made spoke volumes. Yes, my client was definitely in trouble, it meant. We were going to plea-bargain, obviously. No? Now he was starting to look at me with a certain curiosity. What on earth was I planning to do with an open-and-shut case like that? After a moment's hesitation, I told him – omitting a few details – what I was thinking of doing. I told him that Paolicelli claimed he was innocent and had been framed, and that I believed him and wanted to try to get him acquitted.

He listened to me politely, and didn't say anything until I'd finished.

"If your client is telling the truth, then he's really in a tough spot. And I wouldn't like to be in his lawyer's shoes."

I was about to reply that I wouldn't like to be in his lawyer's shoes either, when the hum of the courtroom was interrupted by the sound of the bell. The judges were coming in.

30

The three judges entered after having the bell rung a second time. It wasn't what you'd call a band of youngsters. The youngest – Girardi – was over sixty, and the presiding judge – Mirenghi – was just over a year away from retirement.

The third one – Russo – would normally fall asleep a few minutes after the beginning of a hearing and would wake up when it was time to go. He was quite well known for this, and didn't rank very high in my personal league table of judges.

As far as I was concerned, these three were neither good nor bad. Basically, they liked an easy life, but there were worse appeal court judges. Better ones, too, to tell the truth, but I really couldn't complain.

They quickly got through the cases that had to be adjourned, and a couple of cases involving plea-bargaining, including that of my colleague Castellano. Then Mirenghi asked the clerk of the court if the escort had arrived from the prison with the defendant Paolicelli. The clerk of the court said yes, they had arrived and were waiting in the holding cells.

The holding cells are located in the basement of the courthouse.

Every time I hear them mentioned, I recall the only time I've ever been in them. A client of mine had asked to speak to me urgently before the hearing started. The prosecutor had authorized me to go down with the escort and talk to him down there. My client was a robber who had decided to turn State's evidence, but wanted to talk to me before he took the plunge.

I remember an abstract, secret world. There was a corridor with a defective neon light that went on and off intermittently. On either side, cells that looked like cages for battery animals. Nightmarish ravines from which a clawed hand might suddenly emerge and grab hold of me. A smell of damp, mildew and oil. Muffled, menacing noises. Filthy, peeling walls. A feeling that the normal rules didn't apply down here. That there were other rules, unknown and disturbing.

It struck me that we were only a few yards from the so-called normal world, and I wondered how many other terrifying secret worlds like this one I had come close to in my life.

It wasn't a pleasant sensation and I didn't feel better until I was back in the familiar shabbiness of the courtroom.

*

The guards led Paolicelli to his cage and, once he was inside, took off his handcuffs through the bars. I went up to him to say hello, and as I shook his hand I asked him, as was customary, if we were still agreed about our strategy. Yes, he said, we were agreed. Mirenghi said we could start, I returned to my place, put on my robe, and just before the opening formalities got going I thought of Natsu and her little girl and the walk in the park. And what had happened after that.

Judge Mirenghi read out the preliminary report. It didn't take more than five minutes. Then he turned to me and the assistant prosecutor and asked if by any chance there were any requests for plea-bargaining.

Montaruli opened his hands a little and shook his head. I stood up, adjusting my robe on my shoulders.

"No, Your Honour. We have no requests for plea-bargaining. I do however have a request for new testimony to be considered."

Mirenghi frowned. Girardi looked up from the file he was examining. Russo was looking for the best position in which to doze off and gave no indication that he had heard anything.

"Signor Paolicelli, in accordance with a questionable strategy on the part of his counsel, declined to testify during his original trial. We consider now that this was an erroneous choice. We consider that it is vital for the court to hear the defendant's own story, both as regards the events which form the basis of the charges against him and those which took place subsequently. From the same perspective, and with the same aim, we also request that testimony be heard from Paolicelli's wife, Signora Natsu Kawabata."

I paused for a few moments. Mirenghi and Girardi were listening to me. Russo was slowly tilting to one side. Everything was going well, so far.

"Apart from the request to examine both the defendant and his wife, we also have another request. It is a request I do not make lightly; you will soon understand why. In the last few days my client has revealed to me certain factors pertaining to his relationship with his previous defence counsel, pertaining in particular to the substance of certain conversations with said counsel. According to Signor Paolicelli – as he will of course relate in his testimony – the previous counsel implied to him that he knew the people responsible for the illegal operation for which Paolicelli was first arrested and then sentenced. The significance of such information is obvious, and it will naturally have to be subjected to careful scrutiny as to its reliability. But just as naturally, in order for it to be evaluated, it will have to be elicited from the person directly concerned, that is, Avvocato Macrì. I therefore request that Avvocato Macrì be called as a witness.

"Needless to say, these requests for the admission of new testimony were not anticipated when the appeal was originally drawn up, since this was done by the previous counsel, within the framework of a radically different defence strategy. But as the court will be able to ascertain, they clearly fall within the paradigm laid down in Article 603, Paragraph 3, of the code of criminal procedure. And on the basis of the statements which the defendant will make in his examination, you will be able to verify for yourselves the absolute necessity for the admission of Avvocato Macrì's testimony, as requested."

It was done. Only after I'd finished speaking, when Mirenghi asked the assistant prosecutor to give his response to my requests, did I become fully aware of what I had set in motion.

Quite apart from the written rules – those in the code and in the rulings interpreting that code – there are a great many unwritten rules regarding the conduct of court proceedings, and they're much more strictly obeyed. There's one that goes something like this: a lawyer doesn't defend a client by hanging a colleague out to dry. It isn't done, and that's it. Anyone who violates this rule usually pays for it, one way or another.

Or at the very least, someone tries to make him pay.

Montaruli rose to give his response.

"Your Honour, this seems to me – at least as far as the request to call the previous counsel as a witness is concerned – a somewhat unusual hypothesis on which to base a request for the admission of new testimony. Quite apart from the question of merit, I think there are several legal obstacles to admission of testimony from the former counsel. I shall briefly list these possible legal obstacles. Firstly, if I have understood correctly, from the sketchy indications provided by Avvocato Guerrieri, there seems to be a suggestion that the previous counsel conducted his defence in order to serve interests other than his client's. If this is the case, it would be impossible to examine said counsel as a witness since, ultimately, he would be asked to make statements that might incriminate him. Secondly, I think that there would in any case still be a conflict of interest, according to Article 197 of the code of criminal procedure. Finally, and conclusively, I consider that in any case said counsel could invoke lawyer-client confidentiality in accordance with Article 200. For all these reasons I oppose the admission of testimony from Avvocato Macrì. I have no objections to the other requests regarding the examination of the defendant and his wife."

Mirenghi whispered something in Girardi's ear. He didn't even turn to Russo. I got to my feet and asked permission to speak.

"Your Honour, I'd like to make a few observations on what the assistant prosecutor had just said."

"On what in particular, Avvocato Guerrieri?"

"On the assistant prosecutor's outline of the presumed inadmissibility of Avvocato Macrì's testimony."

"If necessary, you can make these observations at another time. For the moment we agree to the examination of your client and of his wife. We will decide on the other request once these are over."

Then, before I could add anything else, he dictated his ruling to the clerk of the court. "Having considered the admissibility of the examination of the defendant and of his wife, and having considered that it is not possible at the present time to come to a decision as to the admissibility of testimony from Avvocato Macrì, it being necessary to hear said examination in order to evaluate its bearing on this case, the court admits the examination of the defendant and of his wife, and reserves any possible further decision until it has been completed."

All things considered, it was the right thing to do. I would probably have done the same in their place.

Mirenghi again addressed me. "Avvocato Guerrieri, how long do you think the examination of your client will take? If it is something we can get through in a few minutes, we'll proceed now. If not, as we have to close today's session early due to a personal engagement of my own, it would be better to adjourn."

"Your Honour, I don't think it will take long, but I doubt that a few minutes would be enough. It may be better to have a short adjournment."

Mirenghi made no comment on this. He put it on record that the next hearing would take place in a week's time, and then said that there would now be a recess of five minutes.

I was on my way to tell Paolicelli that things were going more or less as I'd expected, when I saw his eyes moving towards the door of the courtroom. I turned and saw Natsu coming in.

I found myself blushing, in a way I hadn't since I was a child. This was the first time, since this whole business had started, that we were all together in the same place. Natsu, her husband and I.

Paolicelli called me. I hesitated for a few moments, hoping the blushing would disappear or at least fade a little, and then walked to the cage.

He wanted to say hello to his wife and needed his guards to let her come closer. I asked Montaruli, and he authorized the defendant and his wife to have a brief conversation. As a rule this isn't done – only a limited number of such conversations are allowed and they can only take place in prison – but in practice prosecutors who aren't complete bastards bend the rules a little during the pauses between cases.

Natsu leaned against the cage and he took her hands through the bars. He squeezed them in his, and said something which luckily I couldn't hear. I felt a twinge of jealousy, and a simultaneous pang of guilt. They were very different but both hurt equally.

I had to leave the courtroom to overcome the feeling that everyone was looking at my face and could see in it what was happening inside me.

A few minutes later the escort passed me, taking Paolicelli away in handcuffs. He greeted me with a kind of weak smile and raised his fettered hands.

31

The afternoon before the second hearing I went to visit Paolicelli in prison. I told him what would happen the following morning – I would begin with his wife's testimony and then I would examine him – gave him advice on how to conduct himself in court, and went over the questions I was going to ask him and the answers he should give me.

It didn't take very long. We finished in less than half an hour.

As I was putting my papers in my briefcase, getting ready to leave, Paolicelli asked me if I didn't mind staying another ten minutes or so for a chat. Those were his exact words: *You couldn't stay another ten minutes or so for a chat?*

I couldn't help the look of surprise on my face, and obviously he noticed.

"I'm sorry. I know it's ridiculous, I don't know what came over me . . ."

I interrupted him with an awkward gesture of the hand, as if to tell him he didn't need to apologize. "It isn't ridiculous. I know how alone you can feel in prison."

He looked me in the eyes, then covered his face with his hands for a few seconds and gave an almost harsh sigh, heavy with suffering but also a kind of relief.

"Sometimes I think I'm going mad. I think I'll never get out of here. I'll never see my little girl again, my wife will meet someone else and make a new life for herself —"

"I met your daughter. Your wife brought her into the office one evening. She's really beautiful."

I don't know why I said that. To interrupt what he was saying, I guess, and make my guilt more bearable. Or maybe there was another reason. Whatever it was, the words just came out, and I couldn't control them.

I couldn't control anything in this situation any more.

He was looking for something to say in reply but couldn't find it. His lips were tight and he was on the verge of tears. I didn't look away, as I would have done as a rule. Instead I reached an arm across the table and put my hand on his shoulder. As I did so, I thought about how many times I'd fantasized about getting my hands on him one day.

None of this makes sense, I thought.

"How do you spend your time in here?" I asked him.

He rubbed his eyes and sniffed before replying. "I'm quite lucky. I work in the infirmary, and that helps. Part of the day passes quickly. Then in my free time . . ."

As he said this, he became aware of the paradox. *Free time.* He seemed about to make a joke out of it, but then must have thought it wouldn't be funny or even original. So he just made a tired gesture and continued talking.

". . . well, anyway, when I'm not working I try to do a little exercise, you know, press-ups, stretching, that kind of thing, and apart from that I read."

Right, I thought. That was the only thing missing. A Fascist who reads. Do they have the works of Julius Evola in the prison library? Or maybe highlights from *Mein Kampf*?

"What do you read?"

"Whatever I can find. Right now I'm reading Nelson Mandela's autobiography, *A Long Road to Freedom.* It's a good title, for someone in my position. Do you like reading, Avvocato?"

I thought of telling him he didn't have to keep calling me Avvocato. It was a bit absurd, considering – how shall I put it? – everything there was and had been between us. Only he didn't know what there was and had been, between all of us. He would probably never know.

"Yes, I like it a lot."

"And what are you reading now?"

I was reading *Nothing Happens by Chance*. And as I answered his question and told him the title I had the feeling that everything suddenly had a clear, distinct meaning. Or rather, that this clear, distinct meaning had always been there, like Poe's purloined letter, but I simply hadn't been capable of grasping it. Because it was too obvious.

His voice dispelled everything before I could find the words to define that meaning and remember it. "Is it a novel?"

"No, it's an essay by a Jungian psychoanalyst. It's about chance and coincidence, and the stories we tell ourselves to give meaning to chance and coincidence. It's a good book, a book about the search for meaning, and about stories." And then, after a brief pause, I added, "I like stories a lot."

Why was I saying these things? Why was I telling him that I liked stories? Why was I talking about myself?

We carried on chatting. A bit more about books, then about sport. He would never have guessed I was into boxing, he said, I didn't really look the type, I didn't even have a broken nose. He himself played tennis, quite well in fact. A pity there weren't any courts in prison – that might have been why his backhand wasn't what it should be. He was more relaxed now and the joke came out quite freely. At that point I remembered that the first time we met he'd told me he'd started smoking again in prison, and yet I'd never seen him light a cigarette.

How come? I asked him. He didn't want to make me feel uncomfortable, he replied, seeing that I'd quit smoking. I said thanks, but smoke didn't make me feel uncomfortable any more. *Almost* never, I thought without saying it. He nodded, but said he'd continue not to smoke when we met. He preferred it that way.

After smoking we got on to music.

"I think music is one of the things I miss the most."

"Do you mean to listen to or to play?"

He smiled, and shrugged slightly. "No, no. To listen to. I'd have loved to learn an instrument, but I never tried. There are a lot of things I've never tried, but there you go. No, I love listening to music. Especially jazz."

"What kind of jazz?"

"Do you like it too?"

"Fairly. I listen to it a lot, though I'm not sure I always understand it."

"I like all kinds of jazz, but here in prison what I miss most is some of the classic tracks I used to listen to when I was young."

You mean when you were a Fascist thug and painted swastikas on walls? Didn't you know that jazz is black people's music? How does that fit in with the master race and crap like that?

"My father was a great jazz fan. He had this incredible collection of old records, including some really rare LPs from the Fifties. They're mine now, and I still have a real turntable to play them on."

That record collection must have been in one of the rooms I didn't go into, I thought, and suddenly the smell of the apartment filled my nostrils, and I felt sad.

"Do you have a favourite piece?"

He smiled again, looking into the distance, and nodded.

161

"Yes, I have. 'On the Sunny Side of the Street'. If I get out of here, one of the first things I'm going to do is listen to a very old radio recording I have of that piece. It was made by Louis Armstrong in the RAI studios in Florence, in 1952, I think. He sings and plays on it. It's a crackly old recording, but it still sends shivers down my spine."

He startling softly whistling 'On the Sunny Side of the Street', perfectly in tune, and for a few moments forgot about me and everything, filling that shabby, silent room with notes, while the questions ricocheted around my head like billiard balls.

Who the fuck are you? Were you really there when that young man was stabbed to death? And are you still a Fascist? How could you have been a Fascist and liked jazz? How can you like books? Who are you?

The music faded away without my even noticing, and with it my thoughts, and my answerless questions. Some of my certainties had already faded away some time previously.

Paolicelli told me I should go. He had taken unfair advantage of my kindness. He was very grateful to me for this chat. He'd really enjoyed it.

I told him I'd enjoyed it, too.

I wasn't lying.

"So, we'll see each other tomorrow in court."

"Tomorrow. And thank you. For everything."

Yes, for everything.

32

I went straight from the prison to my office, where I had an appointment with Natsu. I told her more or less the same things I'd told her husband, about what would happen in court, how she should conduct herself, and so on.

Before going to the prison, before talking to Paolicelli, I'd thought of asking Natsu if we could see each other that evening. But after that conversation, I didn't feel like saying anything.

I felt a mixture of tenderness, shame and nostalgia. I thought how nice it would be if that hard lump of pain deep inside me over Margherita disappeared as if by magic, and how nice it would be if I could just fall in love with Natsu without having to worry about anything. I thought how nice it would be to make plans in my mind for the future, for all the days and nights we could spend together. For many things. It was probably nothing to do with her; it was about the idea of being in love, of playing the game, the idea of a life that wasn't one of resignation.

But it wasn't possible.

So, when we'd finished talking about the case, I simply told her that she was more beautiful than ever, walked around to the front of my desk, kissed her on the cheek, and told her I'd be working late.

She looked at me for a long time, as if she hadn't quite understood. Who could blame her? Then she also kissed me on the cheek and left.

The usual routine followed, just a little more melancholy than usual. Coming back from the office, punchball, shower, roll, beer.

It wasn't a good evening to stay indoors, so I decided to go to the cinema. At an old cinema called the Esedra they were showing Altman's *The Long Goodbye*. It took me twenty minutes to get there, walking quickly through streets so deserted and windswept they were almost scary.

The man in the box office wasn't pleased to see me and made no attempt to conceal the fact. He even hesitated for a few moments to take the banknote I had placed in front of him. I had the impression he was begging me to leave. I must have been the only person there. Without me they could close up early. In the end, he took the money, tore off the ticket and handed it to me, bad-temperedly, along with the change.

I entered the completely empty auditorium. I don't know if the total absence of human sensory stimuli sharpened my sense of smell or if the cinema needed a good cleaning, but I could distinctly smell the upholstery on the seats and the dust that permeated them.

I sat down and looked around. The place was a perfect setting for an episode of *The Twilight Zone*. Indeed, for a few seconds I had to resist the impulse to go and make sure the man in the box office hadn't turned into a giant man-eating crustacean and that the emergency exits hadn't become portals into another dimension.

Then a woman came in. She sat down close to the exit, some ten rows behind me. If I wanted to look at her I had to make a deliberate effort to turn round, which could seem dodgy if I overdid it. So I managed to get only a vague idea of her before the lights went out and the film started. She was of medium height, was wrapped in a large shawl, or maybe a poncho, had very short hair, and seemed to be more or less my age.

During the first half, I didn't pay much attention to the film – I'd already seen it twice anyway. I was thinking I'd like to start up a conversation with that girl, or woman, or whatever she was. I'd like to talk to her in the interval and then, when the film was over, invite her for a drink. As long as she hadn't left during the first half, driven out by the weird atmosphere of that deserted cinema. And by the fear that the only other person there – who had turned round to look at her rather too many times – might be some kind of pervert.

But she was still there in the interval. She had taken off her poncho or shawl and seemed completely at ease, but of course I didn't have the courage to start up a conversation.

During the second half, I thought of a good opening gambit: the presence of the young Arnold Schwarzenegger in the film. Look, there's Schwarzenegger as a young man. Hard to believe he's now the governor of California. All right, it's pretty weak, but for a film buff – and damn it, a woman who goes on her own to see *The Long Goodbye* at that hour of the night must be a film buff – the gambit marked "first appearances of then unknown actors who later became famous" isn't a bad one.

When the lights went on – the projectionist cutting off the end titles abruptly – I stood up, determined to approach her. I had never approached a woman like that in my life, but I was a grown-up now – so to speak – and it was worth a try. Anyway, what was the worst that could happen?

But this time she was gone. The cinema was empty again.

I hurried to the exit, thinking she'd stood up just before the lights went on. But there was no one in the street.

The wind was even stronger now than when I'd arrived, creating eddies of dust. As if in a dream or an apparition, five stray dogs crossed the road in single file and vanished behind a corner.

I turned up my coat collar, stuck my hands in my pockets and went home.

33

The next day I woke up aching all over, and the pains didn't go even after my usual stretches. Needless to say, I wasn't in a good mood as I walked to the courthouse. My mood got worse when I entered the crowded, overheated courtroom and saw that the assistant prosecutor for that hearing was Porcelli.

He was a man with the personality and charisma of a squid. Even physically, wrapped in his robe, with his tall body and small head, he gave the impression of a large, superfluous marine invertebrate. He didn't give a damn about anything. Everything about him conveyed an almost inhuman sense of dull indifference.

At least he wouldn't be a tough opponent, I thought, filing the matter away. The judges were coming in.

*

The bailiff called Natsu, who was waiting in the witness room. She came out and looked around for a few moments, slightly disorientated. The bailiff led her past the judges. Everyone was looking at her.

"Before we begin," Mirenghi said, "I am obliged by law to inform you that as the wife of the defendant you have the right not to testify. However, if you decide not to exercise this right, you are required to tell the truth like any other witness. Do you wish to testify?"

"Yes, Your Honour."

"Very well. Please read the oath."

Natsu took the small laminated card which the bailiff handed her and read in a firm voice, "Conscious of the moral and legal responsibility I assume with my testimony, I swear to tell the whole truth and not to conceal anything of which I have knowledge."

"You may proceed, Avvocato Guerrieri."

"Thank you, Your Honour. Signora Paolicelli, obviously you already know what it is you are here to testify about. So I'll dispense with the preliminaries and ask you if it was you who appointed Avvocato Macrì to defend your husband after he was arrested."

"Yes."

"Did you already know Avvocato Macrì when you decided to appoint him?"

"No."

"Why did you appoint him, then?"

"It was suggested to me that I appoint him."

"By whom?"

Natsu was silent for a few moments, as if to collect her thoughts. "It was the day after my husband's arrest. I was leaving home when a young man came up to me. He told me he had been sent by some friends of my husband and gave me a piece of paper with Macrì's name and mobile phone number on it. He told me I should appoint him as soon as possible and he would sort everything out for my husband."

"What did you reply?"

"I don't remember exactly what I said, I mean the exact words, but I tried to get him to explain."

"Why do you say you *tried*?"

"Because he said he couldn't stay, he had to go. He said

168

goodbye, went over to a car parked about thirty feet away, with another person in it, and drove away."

"Did you take the licence number?"

"No, I didn't even think of it. I was too astonished."

"Did you ever meet him again after that?"

"No."

"Would you be able to recognize him if you saw him again?"

"I think so, but I'm not sure."

"Did you subsequently speak to your husband about this episode?"

"Of course."

"And what did he say?"

"He was even more astonished than I was. He had no idea who this young man was, let alone who sent him."

"I have a few more questions, Signora Paolicelli. Could you tell us the circumstances pertaining to the lifting of the sequestration order on your car?"

"Yes. Avvocato Macrì said he would file a motion to get the car back. He said that since the car was mine and I had nothing to do with the crime, there was no reason why they couldn't let me have it. He did in fact file a motion, and a few days later he told me that the prosecutor had lifted the sequestration order."

"And then what happened?"

"We were talking on the phone and I asked him what I had to do to get my car back. He told me not to worry. He was coming to Bari in a few days and he'd go and fetch the car personally."

"And is that what happened?"

"Yes, he collected it and brought it over to my home."

"One last question, Signora Paolicelli. Did you ever pay Avvocato Macrì?"

"No. He said I didn't need to. He said that when it was all over I could give him a present."

"So you never paid him, never even reimbursed him for his expenses?"

"No."

"Did he ever say that there was someone else taking care of his fee?"

"No, not to me. I think he said it to my husband."

"Thank you. I have no other questions."

Mirenghi asked the assistant prosecutor if he had any questions. He shook his head wearily. Girardi told Natsu that she could go. They all watched her as she walked those few yards to the public benches, and for a few moments I felt an inappropriate sense of pride. Then I reminded myself that I had no reason to feel that, and certainly no right.

*

The guards brought Paolicelli into the courtroom and took up their positions around him, as was the practice. Mirenghi made him repeat his particulars and with absurd punctiliousness had him state that he was a resident of Bari but was currently in custody and that therefore his domicile was the prison. Then he advised him of his right to remain silent and asked him if he intended to exercise this right or if he was willing to undergo examination. The whole ritual.

"I wish to testify, Your Honour."

"You may proceed with your examination, Avvocato Guerrieri."

"Thank you, Your Honour. Signor Paolicelli, my first question is a very simple one. Are you guilty or innocent of the crime with which you are charged and for which you were first arrested and then sentenced?"

"Innocent."

"Would you explain to the court why, after a large quantity of narcotics was discovered in your car, you made the following statement: *I acknowledge that the quantity of forty kilos of cocaine was discovered in my car. Regarding this, I freely declare that the drugs belong to myself alone and that my wife Natsu Kawabata, whose full particulars have been noted in other documents, has no connection whatsoever with this illegal transportation, which is the sole responsibility of the undersigned. I placed the narcotics in the car without my wife's knowledge. I have no intention of naming the persons from whom I acquired the aforementioned quantity of narcotics . . . and so on?"

Paolicelli took a deep breath and shifted on his chair before replying. "I was with my wife and daughter. The customs police said they would have to arrest both of us, because there was no way of knowing which of us the drugs belonged to. We were travelling in the same car, we were husband and wife, it was more than likely that we were in cahoots, that we were accomplices. And so they had to arrest both of us."

"And then what happened?"

"I started to panic. I mean, I was already panicking, but the idea that they could arrest my wife, too, and we'd have to find someone to take care of our daughter, terrified me. I begged them to let my wife go, because she didn't know anything about the drugs."

"Whereas you did?"

"No. But I'd realized that I had no way out, that I was caught up in something beyond my control. So what I wanted first of all was to keep my wife and daughter out of it. I mean, it wasn't my choice. Either they'd arrest both of us or they'd arrest only me."

171

"Go on."

"The customs police told me there was only one way to keep my wife out of it. I had to say that the drugs were mine, only mine, and that I'd been carrying them without her knowledge. That was the only way they'd have a pretext not to arrest her, a reason . . ."

"They'd have a reason they could put on the arrest report as to why they were arresting you and not your wife. Because the car was registered to your wife, wasn't it?"

"Yes, the car is hers."

"So you made that statement, and they let her go and arrested you. At the beginning of this examination, you claimed to be innocent. Is it correct to say that you made that statement solely with the aim of keeping your wife out of this affair?"

"Yes. The drugs weren't mine. I never knew they were in our car until the customs police found them."

"Are you able to explain, or surmise, when the drugs could have been put in your car?"

It was a question which, in theory, the assistant prosecutor could have objected to. It isn't usually possible to ask a witness to express a personal opinion or to make conjectures. But this was a special case, and anyway the giant squid was there in body only. He gave no sign of having noticed. So Paolicelli was able to answer unhindered. He told the whole story of the hotel car park and the keys he'd left with the porter, and how easy it would have been to fill the car with drugs during the night. He answered well, clearly and spontaneously. For what it was worth, he gave the impression of someone who was telling the truth.

Once we had got through the part relating to Montenegro, we went on to Macrì. We briefly recapped the things Natsu had said and then concentrated on the question of what he and his counsel had talked about in the prison.

"What did Macrì say when you asked him who the people were who had approached your wife?"

"He told me not to worry, some friends had asked him to help me."

"Whose friends?"

"I don't know. He said friends, but didn't go into any details."

"But did you have any idea who he was referring to?"

"Absolutely none."

"Do you, or did you, have any friends or acquaintances in common?"

"No."

"Did you ever tell Avvocato Macrì that you were innocent?"

"No."

"Why not?"

"Because I had the impression he knew that perfectly well."

"What gave you that impression?"

"He often said to me, I know you're innocent, it was a bit of bad luck but you'll see, we'll sort everything out. Not in so many words, but that was the sense of it."

"What did Macrì say to you before your first interrogation by the examining magistrate?"

"He told me to exercise my right to remain silent."

"Why?"

"He said there was a risk of making the situation worse. He said I shouldn't worry, he would sort everything out. I just had to be patient."

"Did he tell you that he would get you acquitted?"

"No. He never said that. But he often told me that if I was patient and let him get on with it, he would get me a lower sentence. He said it in a knowing kind of way, as if he knew the right channels . . . I don't know if I'm making myself clear."

"Yes, you're making yourself very clear," I said, looking at the judges. "You trusted completely in this unknown lawyer, who appeared out of the blue in somewhat mysterious circumstances. Can you explain why?"

"I felt – and still feel – as if I was in the middle of something I didn't understand and couldn't control. Macrì seemed to know what he was doing, it seemed as if he knew things . . . I don't know how to put it . . . it seemed as if he really could do what he promised."

"Didn't you know any lawyers you trusted who could have worked with Macrì?"

"I didn't know anyone well enough to trust them. As I said, Macrì had this knowing way about him that —"

Mirenghi broke in. "Please avoid giving us your impressions and personal feelings. If there are facts, then state them, but keep your personal opinions and conjectures to yourself."

"With all due respect, Your Honour, the defendant was explaining why he —"

"Avvocato, I have ruled on this point. Ask another question."

Actually, he'd already said what I'd wanted him to. How useful it would be was another matter. It was time to bring the examination to its conclusion. I asked Paolicelli to talk about his last meeting with Macrì in prison and the quarrel they had had. I'd advised him to tone things down in his account of that meeting, and in particular not to mention Macrì's threats. I wanted to avoid the court refusing to allow

Macrì's testimony on the – perfectly reasonable – grounds that it was impossible to summon someone as a witness and then ask him questions which might oblige him to incriminate himself. That would have brought our case to a premature halt.

Paolicelli was good. He used exactly the right tone, once again implying that there was something not quite above board about Macrì's conduct, but without exaggerating, without explicitly accusing him of anything. When his account of that last meeting was over, I told myself that so far we had done everything we could, as well as we could. The difficult part was coming up now.

Paolicelli was led back to the cage. Mirenghi looked ostentatiously at his watch and turned to me.

"We still have pending your request to call your client's former defence counsel as a witness. Do you still wish this request to be considered, Avvocato Guerrieri?"

I got to my feet, making my usual gesture, almost a tic with me, of pulling my robe up over my shoulders. Yes, I said, I did still wish the request to be considered. Avvocato Macrì's testimony was important to us. Indeed, after the statements we had heard during this hearing, its importance should have been obvious.

Very briefly, I went over the objections the assistant prosecutor had made in the previous hearing, concerning the admissibility of the testimony, and tried to explain why those objections should not be heeded. Then the judges retired to their chamber to make their decision.

34

Mirenghi had said that they would be in their chamber for twenty minutes at the most. They took an hour and a half. I wondered – as I had often done during similar delays – if they were completely incapable of foreseeing how long their work would take them, or if they did it deliberately. As a petty and more or less conscious demonstration of power.

Mirenghi sat down, checked that the clerk of the court was in his seat, cast a glance at me and at the giant squid, just to make sure that we were also there, put on his glasses and read out the ruling.

"Regarding the defence counsel's request to hear further testimony, and having heard the opinion of the assistant prosecutor, the court declares as follows. There are no obstacles of a formal nature to the request to call the defendant Paolicelli's previous defence counsel as a witness. Considering the objections of the prosecution and the subsequent observations of the defence it is possible to state that:

"One. Given the version of the facts presented by the defence, to which we have adhered in evaluating the admissibility of the requests, Avvocato Macrì's testimony must not focus on the conduct of the aforesaid lawyer but on circumstances within his knowledge; within these limits his testimony is admissible;

"Two. There is no conflict of interest as defined in Article 197 of the code of criminal procedure: Avvocato Macrì did not carry out any investigations on behalf of the defence and does not fall within any of the other conditions laid down in said article;

"Three. Lawyer-client confidentiality may be claimed in the course of the testimony but does not constitute a reason for the testimony not to be admitted.

"On this basis the request to call Avvocato Macrì as a witness is therefore considered admissible."

Mirenghi concluded the reading of the judges' ruling with the date of the next hearing and a few further formalities, and then declared that the hearing was adjourned.

As the judges rose to leave I walked to the cage, feeling Natsu's eyes on me. I told Paolicelli it had gone well, we should be pleased. I didn't tell him the thought I'd had a little earlier, after his examination. The difficult part was just starting.

35

The phone call came in the afternoon while I was seeing a client.

Maria Teresa called me on the internal line and, before I had time to tell her that I didn't like to be interrupted when I was seeing a client, she told me it was Avvocato Corrado Macrì, calling from Rome.

I was silent for a few seconds. I remember asking myself, word for word: why the hell didn't it occur to me that he might phone?

"All right, put him through." I covered the receiver with my hand and asked my client – Signor Martinelli, a stolid-looking pensioner whose beautiful little villa, which he'd built without permission in the middle of a protected forest, had been seized by the forest rangers – if he would excuse me for a few minutes, I had an urgent matter to attend to. What I meant was: if he'd be so kind as to leave the room for a few minutes, but he didn't understand. He told me not to worry, I could carry on, and stayed where he was.

"Hello?"

Pause. Noise in the background. He must have been in a car.

Then a deep, rather mellow voice. With a barely noticeable Calabrian accent, much less obvious than I would have expected from my stereotypical image of him.

"Avvocato Guerrieri?"

"Who is that?"

"Your colleague Macrì from Rome."

My colleague, right.

"Go on."

Another pause, a shorter one this time.

"Listen, colleague, I won't beat about the bush. I had a letter from the clerk of the court's office in Bari yesterday. A summons to appear as a witness in the appeal hearing of a man named Paolicelli. I defended him, as I'm sure you know."

Defended was a somewhat loose way of putting it, I'd say. How about saying you really fucked it up for him?

"I found out that you're his counsel now and I wanted to ask you why they summoned me. Was it the prosecutor's doing?"

A barely perceptible hint of anxiety in that mellow voice. He didn't know why he'd been summoned. Which meant he didn't yet know it was me he had to thank for it. The most amusing part of the call was still to come.

"Look, Macrì, we need to clarify a number of details —"

"I'm sorry, Guerrieri, but who is 'we'?"

The hint of anxiety had become an aggressive under-current.

"My client and I —"

"Your client and you? You mean Paolicelli? Are you telling me it was you who asked for me to be summoned?"

"As I was saying, we need to clarify a number of things –"

"What the fuck are you saying? You had me called? Me, a colleague?"

This was it. We'd got past the hints now. Instinctively, I pressed the receiver to my ear and glanced at my client. He was looking with vague interest at a framed reproduction of a Domenico Cantatore painting I had hung in my office a few weeks earlier.

"Look, I'm not accustomed to talking to someone who raises his voice to me" – it struck me that I was talking complete bullshit – "and anyway I don't think it's a good idea to continue this conversation. I'm representing my client in an appeal in which, whether you like it or not" – I felt a wicked little pleasure in uttering those words: *whether you like it or not* – "you have to appear as a witness. When you appear in court —"

"Appear in court? Are you completely stupid?" He was almost choking with rage now. "Have you got shit for brains? Do you really think I'm going to appear before some fucking court of appeal? Get this into your thick head. I'm fucked if I'm going to come to Bari and go through all that crap."

For a few moments I was silent, torn between two kinds of answer. Then I took a deep breath and replied in an apparently calm tone, "I don't think it would be a very good idea if you didn't appear. If you're not in court on the day of the hearing I'll ask the presiding judge to have you brought in by the *carabinieri*. I hope you've got the idea by now."

Silence. Background noise. I thought I heard his laboured breathing, but maybe I was only imagining it. Just as I briefly imagined the homicidal thoughts that must be passing through his head. I decided to take advantage of the situation.

"Now if you'll excuse me, I'm with a client."

That woke him up. He said that I hadn't realized who I was dealing with, and that I had to be very careful. That was the last thing I heard before I slammed the phone down on him, not entirely in control of myself. Like someone who closes the door behind him to escape a pursuer.

"Is everything all right, Avvocato?" my client asked me,

with a gleam of curiosity and even a hint of anxiety on his stolid face.

"Everything's fine," I replied, and had to make an effort not to tell him all about it. I knew that would only be a way of putting a brave face on it.

Everything's fine. Like hell it was. I noticed that my hands were shaking and I had to put them down on the desk and keep them there to avoid making an exhibition of myself in front of Signor Martinelli.

What the hell was I getting myself into?

36

Leaving my office that evening, I looked around. Right, left, and then a glance at the doorway of the old building opposite, just in case the killer sent by Macrì was hiding inside, waiting for me to appear.

Then I shrugged my shoulders and started walking.

I was about ready for the psychiatric hospital, I said to myself under my breath in an attempt to downplay the situation. But I really wasn't in a good mood. I hated that feeling of not being safe, of being vulnerable. But what could that bastard do to me anyway? He couldn't really have me shot. Or could he? He'd kicked up a fuss because he was scared of getting into trouble. Obviously he had something to fear. And what do Mafiosi do when they have something to fear? They react, obviously.

These disjointed thoughts kept going through my head until I reached home, by which time I was bored with them. I'm lucky that way. I can get bored with anything. Even fear. What the hell, I thought, Macrì and his friends could all go fuck themselves.

Anyway, the next day, whatever happened, I would call Tancredi.

37

Tancredi was giving evidence in court that morning. The usual kind of case: a sexual assault on a little girl.

Usual. A nice adjective for something like that.

Sometimes I wondered how Carmelo had managed to cope all this time, dealing with that kind of filth every day. On the few occasions when I'd represented abused children, I'd felt as if I was walking in the dark down corridors filled with insects and other repulsive creatures. You can't see them, but they're there, you can sense them moving close to your feet, you can smell them, you can feel something sticky on your face.

I'd once asked him how he did it.

When I asked the question, a kind of deep, metallic glow flashed across his face. It was a fleeting thing, barely perceptible, almost scary.

Then everything went back to normal. He pretended to think about my question and gave me a trite answer. To the effect that somebody had to do it, that not many policemen wanted to work in that squad, and so on.

I entered the courtroom. Tancredi was on the witness stand and a fat young lawyer I didn't know was cross-examining him.

I sat down to wait for him and, incidentally, to enjoy the show.

"When you were answering the assistant prosecutor's

questions you said, among other things, that my client *would lurk in the vicinity of the school.* Could you explain to us what you mean by *lurking*? You used a very specific expression and I'd like you to justify it. What was the defendant doing? Was he hiding behind cars, was he using binoculars, or what?"

The fat man finished the question with a little smile. I'm sure he had to make an effort to stop himself casting a knowing glance at his client, who was sitting next to him.

Tancredi looked at him for a few moments. He seemed to hesitate, as if he was searching for an answer. I knew perfectly well that he was acting. That apparently innocent expression was the expression of a cat about to catch a mouse. A *big* mouse, to be precise.

"Yes. The suspect, that is, the defendant, always reached the school about twelve-twenty and took up a position on the opposite corner. The children would come out a few minutes later. He would watch them come out, and stay there until they'd all left."

"Always on the other side of the street."

"Yes, I already said that."

"He never crossed the road and approached any of the children?"

"Not during the week we were watching him. Subsequently, we discovered other evidence —"

"I'm sorry, but for the moment we're interested in what you saw, or *didn't* see, during that week. Is there a bar near that school?"

"Yes, a bar called Stella di Mare."

"During the time that you were watching him, did my client ever go into that bar?"

"Obviously I wasn't personally on duty all the time, but as far as I remember, I saw him go into that bar a couple of times. Both times, he stayed there for a few minutes and left just as the children were coming out of school."

"You do know, Inspector, that my client is a salesman, dealing with foodstuffs and other products for bars."

"Yes."

"Do you know if the manager of the Stella di Mare is a customer of the defendant?"

"No."

"Can you rule out the possibility that my client was in the vicinity of the school and the bar for reasons connected with his work, rather than those you have surmised in your report and your testimony?"

He was sure he had landed the killer blow.

"Yes," Tancredi replied simply.

The lawyer was stunned. He seemed to have been thrown almost physically off balance. "Yes, what?"

"Yes, I can rule it out."

"Indeed? And why is that?"

"You see, Avvocato, we followed Signor Armenise for several days. We followed him even when he was working, when he went into bars and restaurants for reasons connected with his work. He always had with him a leather briefcase and one of those binders in which you can insert and remove pages. You know, the kind that salesmen use to show the range of their products. On the occasions when we observed him outside the school he never had either his case or his binder with him."

"I'm sorry, but when Signor Armenise entered the Stella di Mare, were you or any of your subordinates inside the bar, so that you could hear the conversations he had with the manager?"

"No. We were on the other side of the street."

"So it's on the basis of mere conjecture that —"

The assistant prosecutor intervened. "Objection, Your Honour. Counsel for the defence cannot make statements that are offensive to the witness."

The fat man was about to reply but the presiding judge got in first. "Avvocato, please confine yourself to asking questions. Any comments you may wish to make you may leave for your closing argument."

"Very well, Your Honour. So, is it correct to say that during the week that you were watching Signor Armenise you didn't gather any evidence to confirm the complaints you'd received?"

"No, I wouldn't say that was correct. When parents report that someone is molesting their children close to a school, and I then discover that this person is in the habit of standing outside another school when the children are coming out, for me that *is* evidence to confirm the reports. Obviously if, during the course of the investigations, we actually witnessed a sexual assault being committed, as sometimes happens, we would then arrest the person involved. But that's another matter."

The fat man tried again to argue that these were personal opinions, but this time there wasn't even any need for the assistant prosecutor to intervene. The presiding judge asked him, in a not very friendly tone, if he had any other questions relating to the *facts* of the case. If not, the cross-examination could be considered closed. The man stammered inaudibly and sat down. The assistant prosecutor had no more questions for Tancredi, so the judge thanked him and told him he could go.

*

"Let's get out of here if we want a coffee," Tancredi said. So we left the courthouse and set off through the streets of the Libertà. As we walked I told him about the latest developments, especially the phone call from my friendly colleague. Tancredi listened without making any comments, but when I told him that Macrì had threatened me, he gave a quick grimace.

"What are you thinking of doing?" he asked me. We were having coffee in a bar frequented by smugglers, whores, lawyers and policemen.

I didn't like the question. It seemed like a way of asking me if I was thinking of dropping the case.

I replied that there wasn't much to think about. If Macrì came to court the day he had been summoned to appear, I would examine him and try to extract some evidence useful to my client. If he didn't come, I would ask for him to be brought to court by the *carabinieri*, and yes, I knew perfectly well he would go crazy, but I couldn't do anything about that.

"But you can still give me a hand."

"You want police protection when the Calabrian Mafia send their hitmen to get you, is that it?"

"Very funny. I need some more information about this Macrì."

"What kind of information?"

"Something to use when I examine him. Something I can spring on him to try and wrongfoot him. Bear in mind that I'm going into this more or less blind. If he sounds convincing I've lost the case."

Tancredi stopped, lit a cigar, and looked me in the eyes. "Well, you've really got nerve, I'll say that for you."

I didn't say anything. I knew he was right.

187

38

The next day Tancredi stopped by the office.

He came into my room, sat down and looked at me without saying anything.

"Well?"

"I don't know if you're lucky, or the opposite."

"What do you mean?"

"Do you know what accommodation records are?"

"To be honest, no. Should I?"

"They're the records kept in the databank of the Ministry of the Interior, where all overnight stays in hotels and boarding houses, and all apartment rentals, are registered. I did a search for our friend Macrì, and guess what I found?"

"I'm sure you're about to tell me."

"Granted that Signor Macrì travels a lot – there are a lot of entries in his name – I found that he's often stayed at hotels in Bari. Both before and after Paolicelli was arrested. The times after the arrest don't matter very much. The others are more interesting. And two of these in particular are extremely interesting."

"Why?"

"Guess who stayed in the same hotel on the same two nights."

"I'm stupid. Who?"

"Luca Romanazzi. And the same Romanazzi slept in the same hotel the night after Paolicelli was arrested."

Shit. I didn't say that, but I made a noise as I thought it. "That *is* interesting."

"Right. Now, though, you have to find a way to use it."

"How do you mean?"

"Well, you can't say a friend of yours, a police inspector, did an unauthorized search in the Ministry of the Interior database on your behalf."

"Right."

"Find a way to make him admit it when you question him. Make him think you hired a private detective to look at the hotel registers. Make up any story you like."

"Thanks, Carmelo."

He nodded, as if to say, you're welcome, but I really don't know how much good this'll do you. Silently, he placed on the desk the sheets of paper he'd been holding in his hand until then.

"Memorize what's written here and then throw these papers away. Technically, they're evidence of an offence."

39

The afternoon before the hearing in which we were due to hear Macrì's testimony I didn't even touch the file. I concentrated on other things entirely. I wrote out an appeal which wasn't actually due for another week. I made out a few bills for clients who were late paying. I updated some out-of-date files.

Maria Teresa realized that something wasn't quite right, but was wise enough not to ask any questions. When it was time to close the office and she put her head in to say goodbye, I asked her to order me the usual pizza and beer.

I didn't get down to work until after nine. That's typical of me. I'm a specialist in leaving things until the last minute. If a task is difficult, or important, or possibly both, I tend to deal with it only when the water is already up to my neck, or even a little higher.

I reread all the papers in the file. There weren't many of them. I also reread all my notes. Not many of those either. I started to jot down a series of questions. I wrote about twenty of them, according to the strategy I proposed following, as some of the manuals suggest. But then I felt a fool, and I was sure I would feel a fool reading out those questions when I examined Macrì.

You don't prepare for a fight, I told myself, by writing out a list of the punches and dodges and moves you're thinking of making in the ring, from the first bell to the last. It doesn't work like that. In the boxing ring or in court. Or in life.

As I crumpled up my stupid list of questions and threw it

in the waste-paper basket, I recalled the world heavyweight title fight between Muhammad Ali and George Foreman in Kinshasa in 1974.

The most extraordinary fight in the history of boxing.

In the days before the fight, Foreman had said he would knock Ali out in two or three rounds. He was certainly capable of it. He started the fight punching like a madman. It looked as if this wasn't going to be a long contest, couldn't be a long contest. Ali tried to dodge, defended himself, was pushed back onto the ropes, and took a lot of punches to his body, punches as heavy as stones.

Without reacting.

And yet he was talking. No one could hear what he was saying, but it was clear to everyone that in the middle of that torrent of violence unleashed by Foreman, Ali's lips were moving constantly. He didn't look like someone who's taking a lot of punches and losing the game.

Contrary to all the forecasts, Ali didn't get knocked out in the first rounds, or the later rounds either. Foreman kept on hitting him furiously, but his blows were having less and less effect. Ali continued dodging, defending himself, taking the blows. And talking.

In the middle of the eighth round, with Foreman now breathing from his mouth and having to make an effort to lift his arms after hundreds of ineffectual punches, Ali suddenly came off the ropes and landed an incredible combination of two-handed blows. Foreman went down, and by the time he got up again the fight was over.

I closed the file and put it in my briefcase. Then I looked among my CDs for a Bob Dylan collection I remembered leaving in the office. It was there. And among the songs on it was 'Hurricane'.

I turned out the light, put on the CD, went and sat down in my swivel chair, my feet crossed on the desk.

I listened to the song three times. Sitting in the half-light, thinking about many things.

Thinking that sometimes I was glad to be a lawyer.

Thinking that sometimes what I did really had something to do with justice. Whatever the word meant.

Then I turned out the light and went home. To sleep, or try to.

40

I was outside the courtroom just before ten. As I approached, I'd felt a slight change of rhythm in my heartbeat and a tingling in my throat. As if my pounding heart was about to trigger a coughing fit. That used to happen to me sometimes when I was at university, in the last days leading up to an important exam.

I looked around for Macrì, even though I had no idea what he looked like. But all the people who were there, outside the courtroom, were people I knew, at least by sight. The usual fauna of lawyers, bailiffs, trainees and secretaries.

On the way to the courthouse I'd had a bet with myself on what would happen. Looking around again just before I entered the courtroom I told myself I had lost. Obviously he hadn't believed in my threat to have him brought in by the *carabinieri*.

I put my briefcase and robe down on the bench. I hoped I wouldn't have to have Macrì brought in like that. I wondered who the assistant prosecutor would be for this hearing.

Then, as if someone had called me, I turned to the door of the courtroom and saw Macrì. I don't know how, but I knew straight away it was him, even though he didn't correspond at all to the physical stereotype I'd imagined on the way to the courthouse: a man of medium height, slightly overweight, with a dark complexion, very black hair, and maybe a moustache.

Corrado Macrì was fair-haired, taller than me and much more robust. Over six feet tall and weighing at least two hundred and twenty pounds, he looked like someone who doesn't have an ounce of fat, lives on protein-filled milkshakes and spends a lot of time lifting weights.

He was very well dressed – anthracite-grey suit, regimental tie, raincoat over his arm – and considering his size his clothes must have been made to measure.

He came straight up to me. He had an agile way of walking, like an athlete in good shape.

A disquieting thought quickly crossed my mind. How had he known it was me? Who had told him?

"Guerrieri?"

"Yes?"

He held out his hand, taking me by surprise. "I'm Macrì," he said with a smile. I suspected he was attractive to women – at least some women – and was well aware of it.

I replied to his handshake and, despite myself, to his smile. I couldn't help it. The man had something about him that made you warm to him. I knew perfectly well who he was – a trafficker disguised as a lawyer – and yet I couldn't avoid finding him oddly likeable.

"We've already spoken on the phone," he said, and smiled again. He looked and sounded quite apologetic.

"Yes," I replied. Not knowing exactly what to say. I couldn't figure out this situation at all.

"We got off to rather a . . . let's say, rather a shaky start. Probably my fault."

This time I didn't even say yes. I simply nodded. That seemed to be the only thing I could manage.

He paused for a few seconds. "Shall we go for a coffee?"

I would have liked to say no, thanks, better not. The

194

hearing's about to start, it's better if we don't go too far away. And don't forget I have to examine you and ask you some rather embarrassing questions. I don't think this is the time or place to become too chummy.

All right, I said, we could have a coffee, the judges wouldn't be here for another fifteen or twenty minutes.

We left the courtroom and as we walked towards the bar, I noticed a man following a few yards behind us. I turned to look at him, wondering who he was.

"Don't worry, Guerrieri. He's my driver. He's keeping his distance because he knows we have to talk and he's very discreet. He knows the score."

As he said these last words – *he knows the score* – the inflexion of his voice changed significantly. From that moment on, I started to take notice of the *carabinieri* dotted around the courthouse. The fact that there were so many of them reassured me. A little, anyway.

"All courthouses are the same. The same chaos, the same smell, the same faces. Right, Guerrieri?"

"I don't know, I've never thought about it."

We reached the basement, made our way through the peak-hour crowds, and had our coffees. Macrì paid and we went out again. The man who knew the score was still behind us.

"Guerrieri, let me tell you this again. I think we got off on the wrong foot in that phone call. I said some things I shouldn't have said to a colleague. You're only doing your job. So am I, come to that."

I nodded, wondering where he was going with this.

"Since you're doing your job, I don't want to give you any trouble. But you shouldn't give me any either."

"What do you mean?"

195

"Look, the hearing is starting, what kind of things do you need to ask me?"

I shouldn't have answered him. I should have said he'd find out soon enough. Once he was on the witness stand. Instead, I told him I needed to clarify certain points about how his relationship with Paolicelli had started. I realized I was being almost apologetic, and I didn't like that at all.

I felt like an idiot.

He looked suddenly intense, in a way that was hardly warranted by my unremarkable answer. He pretended to think about what he was going to say and then, still walking, took my arm.

"Listen to me, Guerrieri. Obviously I'll only answer questions that don't force me to violate lawyer-client confidentiality. There are some I won't be able to answer at all, but you know that, right? But that's not the important thing. There are people who want to take care of Paolicelli. Forget about whether he's innocent or guilty. He's in prison, and he's going to stay there for a while, even though you're working very hard on his behalf. Which is good, it does you credit. It means you're a real professional."

He stopped for a moment to look me in the face. To see if I was taking in what he was saying. I don't know if he got the impression from my face that I was following him, but he continued anyway.

"He has a wife – a beautiful wife, I don't know if you've met her – and a daughter. He's in trouble and needs help. He needs money. He's bound to get a decent reduction on his sentence on appeal, you'll see. Then in a few years he'll get time off for good behaviour. But in all that time, a bit of financial help – *real* financial help – wouldn't go amiss, right?"

"No, it wouldn't go amiss," I answered involuntarily.

He smiled, turning his head slightly towards me. That answer must have given him the idea that we were starting to understand each other. At last. I was someone who knew the ways of the world, who knew the score.

"Good. Naturally it's something you and I have to talk about. Right now, we have to talk about it and sort it out. Don't think I've come empty-handed." So saying, he touched his jacket where the inside pocket was. "And of course we won't forget you. All the work you've done, the time you've put in on this case. And don't forget, these people – the ones I'm talking about, who want to take care of our client – often need lawyers. Good lawyers like you. A sound professional can make a lot of money from certain clients. Obviously you know what I'm talking about, right?"

He kept saying: *right?* It may have had an implied question mark, but it wasn't a question.

Questions came flooding through my mind, uncontrollably. How much easier it would be. Money for him, obviously money for me. How much money do you have in that jacket? How much money can a sound professional like me make? I couldn't block out these obscene questions. Paolicelli inside for a few years. A few more years.

Me outside.

Natsu and the little girl outside, with me.

Someone who knows the score. The phrase came back to me. But it no longer referred to Macrì's henchman. It was the new definition of Guido Guerrieri, the good lawyer. Ready to sell a client for money, love and the crumbs of a life he hadn't been able to make for himself.

Ready to steal another man's life.

It lasted a few seconds, I think. Maybe a little more.

I've rarely, if ever, felt such self-disgust.

Macrì noticed that something was wrong. I was standing there, a strange expression on my face, without answering his question.

"I've made myself clear, right?"

I told him he'd made himself very clear, yes. Then for a few moments I searched for an appropriate one-liner, but couldn't find one. So I just said that we'd consider his generous offer if the original sentence was upheld.

Thinking about it now, maybe *that* was an appropriate one-liner. He stopped and looked at me, questioningly. He was trying to understand. If I was stupid, if I was making idiotic wisecracks, if I was mad.

He couldn't figure it out from my face, and when he started speaking again, his tone had changed. "Very funny. But since the hearing is about to start, I think we ought to talk seriously. I have here with me —"

"You're right, the hearing is about to start. I have to be in court."

I made as if to turn, but he put his big hand on my arm to hold me back. I noticed *the man who knew the score* taking a few steps towards us. I moved my arm away and looked him in the eyes.

"Be careful, Guerrieri."

"Careful about what?"

"This is a game in which people can get badly hurt."

I was calm now. "That's more like it," I replied in a low voice, almost a whisper. "I like you better this way. The role suits you."

"Be careful," he repeated, "or I'll destroy you."

I'd been waiting my whole life for someone – someone like him – to use that line on me. "Just try," I replied.

Then I turned and walked towards the courtroom.

41

Mechanically, I greeted the assistant prosecutor – the giant squid again – and then, after putting on my robe and sitting down, I kept my eyes obstinately fixed on the judges' bench. I kept them fixed there when the judges hadn't yet come in and kept them fixed there – on the wood of the bench, not on the judges – even when they had entered and the hearing had started. I didn't turn round.

I wondered what the various shades of the wood were called. I wondered what had caused the black stains where the grains crossed. I wasn't thinking about anything else. I imagine it was a kind of mental self-defence. I was emptying my mind, and keeping it empty, to hold back the fear.

Like in boxing. The only thing in my life which has always provided me with pearls of wisdom, meaningful images, metaphors.

I broke off for just a few seconds, to wave back at Paolicelli, who had waved to me as the escort brought him into the courtroom. Then I turned back to the patterns of the wood on the judges' bench.

I was concentrating so hard on the grains of the wood that I didn't hear Judge Mirenghi. Or rather, I was in such a trance that I heard his voice in the distance, as if it was something that didn't concern me.

"Avvocato Guerrieri, are you with us?" he asked, raising his voice slightly. A polite reminder that this was his courtroom and not a temple for Zen meditation.

"Yes, Your Honour, I'm sorry. I was just gathering my thoughts and —"

"All right, all right. Are you ready to begin examining the witness you asked to be summoned?"

"Yes, Your Honour."

"Strictly speaking, the court should examine him first, given that this testimony is being admitted according to Article 603, Paragraph 3 of the code of criminal procedure, but I think we can spare ourselves this formality and let you begin, since you have a specific idea of what to ask the witness. If the parties agree, of course."

The parties agreed. Or rather, I agreed and the assistant prosecutor was somewhere else. And had been for at least ten years.

Mirenghi told the bailiff to call the witness Corrado Macrì.

He came in with his raincoat over his arm, nodded politely to the judges, sat down and calmly read the oath. He seemed enormously confident and composed.

"You are a lawyer, so I don't need to explain anything to you," Mirenghi said. "Counsel for the defence has requested that you be examined about certain specific elements of this case and will now address his questions to you. Naturally, if with regard to some of the questions you consider you have to invoke lawyer-client confidentiality, considering the part you played in the previous phases of this case, please do so and we will rule on the matter. Is that all right?"

"Yes, Your Honour, thank you."

Mirenghi turned to me and told me I could proceed. Macrì was staring straight ahead.

200

I looked him in the face for a few moments. This was it, I told myself.

"Avvocato Macrì, were you Signor Paolicelli's defence counsel at his original trial?" A completely unnecessary question, given that this had already been established. But I had to start somewhere.

He answered it straight, without trying to be sarcastic. "Yes."

"When did you first meet Signor Paolicelli?"

"When I visited him in prison for the first time."

"Do you remember when that was?"

"I don't remember the exact date, but he'd been arrested two days earlier and was due to be interviewed by the examining magistrate. That should make it easy enough to work out the date. Assuming it's of any importance."

There was just a hint of aggression in his voice. I ignored his attempt to be provocative. Macrì was still looking straight ahead of him.

"Was it Signor Paolicelli who appointed you?"

"No, it was Signor Paolicelli's wife."

"Do you know Signor Paolicelli's wife?"

"I met her after I was appointed, on my second visit to Bari, when there was a hearing to appeal the arrest. All this is in the documents."

"Do you know why Signora Paolicelli appointed you?"

"I think you have to ask Signora Paolicelli."

"Right now I'm asking you. Do you know why —"

"I can only surmise that some acquaintance of hers gave her my name. You're a lawyer, you know how these things work."

"Let me see if I've understood this correctly. You are appointed by someone you don't know, in a city two hundred and fifty miles from where you're based . . . By the way, you practise in Rome, right?"

"Yes."

"Have you always practised in Rome?"

I was looking right at him, and noticed that his jaw clenched when I asked that question. He must have assumed I was going on to ask him about his misadventures with the police. It's not as simple as that, my friend. The grilling has a long way to go yet, you son of a bitch, I thought, and the words *son of a bitch* echoed in my head.

"No."

"All right. Let's recap: you are appointed by a woman you don't know, who lives in Bari, a long way from where you work. It's an urgent case: her husband has just been arrested on a very serious charge. You rush to Bari, make contact with the husband, agree to defend him, and on your second visit you also meet his wife. And yet you never think to ask why she appointed you, and don't even broach the subject with either the client's wife or the client. Is that correct?"

He paused for about twenty seconds, pretended to think it over. "It may be that we talked about it. I don't recall, but it's possible. They may have told me that someone who knew me gave them my name."

"Had you previously had any other clients in Bari?"

"Probably, I don't remember now."

"Does that mean you have a lot of clients?"

"A fair number, yes."

"You have a prosperous practice."

"I can't complain."

"How many people work in your office?"

"I have a secretary. Apart from that I've always preferred to work alone."

I bet your secretary is the minder you've got with you, right?

"What's the address of your office?"

Mirenghi intervened. Quite rightly.

"Avvocato Guerrieri, what does the address of the witness's office have to do with the case we are hearing?"

I thought I caught a very slight movement on Macrì's face, like the beginnings of a wicked smile.

"Your Honour, I realize this question may seem rather strange. But it's a detail that will help me to clarify other things that are more immediately pertinent to the case."

Mirenghi rolled his eyes imperceptibly. Girardi seemed to be following proceedings closely. Russo – and this was the odd thing – hadn't fallen asleep yet.

"Go on, Avvocato. But please remember we have other cases scheduled for today's session, and we would like to see our families eventually."

"Thank you, Your Honour."

I turned back to Macrì. The vague smile had vanished. Perhaps I'd only imagined it anyway. "Will you tell us the address of your office . . . and while we're about it, the telephone number and fax number."

This time he turned to me before answering. There was genuine hatred in his eyes. Just try, I said inside my head. Just try, you son of a bitch.

He told me the address of his office, hesitated a moment – I was probably the only person to notice – then said that he didn't have a landline, because he preferred to use his mobile for everything.

"Let me see if I've got this straight. You don't have a landline, so obviously you don't have a fax either?"

"As I've said" – he was articulating his words clearly now,

and the effort he was making to control his irritation was more noticeable – "I prefer to use my mobile for everything. We have computers, we're connected to the internet, so instead of faxes, we use the computer and a printer."

He turned to Mirenghi.

"Your Honour, I don't know where Avvocato Guerrieri is planning to go with all this, and I'm not even particularly interested. I must say, though, that I am struck by his unduly aggressive and intimidating tone. I don't think that's the way to speak to a colleague . . ."

"All right, Avvocato Macrì. I think we could spend many hours trying to interpret Avvocato Guerrieri's tone without reaching any agreement. The questions he's asked so far have all been admissible and, in the opinion of the court, have not been prejudicial to the dignity of the witness, that is, you. If you think otherwise, you can complain to the bar council. Avvocato Guerrieri may proceed, as long as he takes into account the warning I gave him before and the fact that we would like to get to the point as soon as possible."

Mirenghi was getting irritated by Macrì. That wasn't necessarily a good thing. When he was irritated, he tended to take it out on anyone within striking distance, no matter who had originally caused the irritation. I knew I'd better get a move on.

"If I understood correctly, you told us that you haven't always practised in Rome, right?" I realized I was saying "right?" at the end of every question, as he had done a while earlier, when we were talking in the corridors.

"I know perfectly well where you're going with this."

"I'm pleased to hear it. If that's the case, perhaps I can spare myself the bother of actually asking you any questions. Would you tell us where you practised before you moved to Rome, and why, and under what circumstances, you moved?"

"I practised in Reggio Calabria, and moved for very personal reasons, sentimental reasons, if you know what I mean."

"I see. But did anything happen to —"

He interrupted me, speaking quickly. "There were charges against me and I was acquitted, for the simple reason that I was innocent. But that has nothing to do with my move to Rome."

At this point I glimpsed Porcelli out of the corner of my eye. He seemed to have come to life a little and was showing a naïve interest in what was happening.

"Was your personal freedom restricted in any way?"

"Yes."

"Were you under house arrest, did you spend time in prison, or what?"

"I was arrested and then, as I said – but I'm sure you already know this – I was cleared of all the charges. Because, I repeat, I was innocent."

"Can you tell us what you were charged with?"

"I was charged with criminal conspiracy in connection with Mafia drug trafficking. The charge was completely without foundation, and I received compensation from the State for unlawful detention. Just to bring your information up to date."

I was about to ask him on what basis he had been arrested and then cleared. But I knew Mirenghi wouldn't let me go that far and even if I did I might jeopardize everything. It was time to get to the point.

"Did you ever tell Signor Paolicelli that you *knew* he was innocent?"

"I may have done. We say a lot of things to our clients, especially the ones who complain the most, who can't stand prison. Signor Paolicelli was like that. Always complaining, I remember."

"Could you tell us what you and Signor Paolicelli talked about? First of all, how many times did you meet?"

"I don't remember how many times we met, five, six, seven. But I will tell you now, out of respect for the dignity of our profession, that I have no intention of talking about the conversations I had with my client, however significant they may be. With regard to these questions, I reserve the right to remain silent, on the grounds of lawyer-client confidentiality."

Mirenghi turned to me, and gave me a questioning look.

"Your Honour, I believe that the rule of lawyer-client confidentiality is there to guarantee that the lawyer can exercise his profession freely, but more specifically to protect the client. It is not a personal privilege for individual lawyers. I'll try to explain. The law allows defenders the right to remain silent as to what they have learned in a professional context, yes, but there is a specific reason for that. It is to guarantee the *client* as much freedom as possible to confide in his own defence counsel, without fear that the latter might subsequently be obliged to disclose the substance of these conversations. That, in a nutshell, is the reason for this right. It's a way of protecting the client and the confidentiality of his relationship with his counsel, and not an indiscriminate privilege for lawyers."

All three judges were listening to me. Russo was looking at me, and his face seemed – how shall I put this? – different.

"If this outline is correct, as I believe it is, then the right to remain silent on the grounds of lawyer-client confidentiality becomes invalid if the client, whose protection this rule is intended for, declares that he releases his counsel – or his former counsel – from the obligation to observe confidentiality. In this instance, Signor Paolicelli – as you will be able to confirm immediately – releases Avvocato Macrì from this obligation. Once you have established that such is the case, I ask you to declare the right to remain silent unfounded and I ask you to order the witness to answer my questions."

"Your Honour," Macrì said, "I'd like to make some observations on what Avvocato Guerrieri has said."

"Avvocato Macrì, you are here as a witness and are not entitled to make observations on anything the parties have said. Signor Paolicelli, do you confirm that you release your former counsel from the right to remain silent regarding the conversations which took place between you and which had as their subject the facts of this case?"

Paolicelli confirmed this. Mirenghi told Macrì to go back into the witness room. Then the three judges rose and retired to their chamber.

I stood up, too, and as I did so I turned and noticed that both Tancredi and Natsu were in the courtroom, sitting a few seats from each other.

42

Natsu stood up. I went up to her and shook her hand. It was a bit of a show. I could feel the eyes of the world on me, Paolicelli's in particular. I held her hand for a very brief moment, but avoided looking in her eyes.

Then I asked her to excuse me because I had to talk to someone. As I walked towards Tancredi I noticed that *the man who knew the score* had vanished. Which made me feel both relieved and anxious in a new kind of way.

"What are you doing here?" I asked.

"I had to go to the Prosecutor's Department. But then I got through my business quicker than I'd expected, so, seeing as how you've involved me in this case anyway, I came to see what was happening. What do you think the judges will do? Will they order him to answer?"

"I don't know. And I don't know which is better for us, to tell the truth."

"What do you mean?"

"If the judges order him to answer and he lies without contradicting himself too much, then it's Paolicelli's word against his."

"And what if they say he can claim lawyer-client confidentiality?"

"I can make something of that in my closing argument. You saw, Your Honours, that the witness Macrì refused to tell us about his conversations with his former client. He claimed lawyer-client confidentiality. Of course he was entitled to do so, in accordance with your order. But we have to ask: why? Why, when his client himself wanted him to talk about the substance of those conversations, did he refuse to do so? Obviously because there was information it wasn't in his interest to reveal."

Having got the technical explanation out of the way, I thought it might be a good idea to tell him about the henchman Macrì had brought with him. "In any case, Signor Macrì didn't come on his own."

Tancredi turned his head slightly, to inspect the courtroom. Macrì's friend had gone, however, so I told him what had happened before the hearing.

"I'm going to call some of my people now. When Macrì's finished on the witness stand we'll put a tail on your pleasant colleague and his friend. If they leave by car we'll have them stopped on the autostrada by the transport police. It'll look like a random check; that way they won't suspect anything. If they take a plane, we'll alert our colleagues in the border police. We'll be able to identify them and see if this man is only a driver and flunkey or something worse."

That made me feel a whole lot better, I thought.

"That way," Tancredi went on, "if anyone does bump you off, you can rest assured it won't go unpunished. Those two will be the first people we arrest."

I don't know why, but I didn't find the joke all that funny. I was looking for an effective retort when the bell rang and the judges came back into the courtroom.

43

Judge Mirenghi read out the ruling with the air of someone who thinks that a certain matter is dragging on and wants everyone else to realize it.

"Having taken note of the witness's declaration that he wishes to exercise the right to lawyer-client confidentiality regarding all questions pertaining to his conversations with the defendant Fabio Paolicelli while functioning as his counsel; having taken note of the statement by the defendant and the observations of his present counsel, who has requested that the witness be ordered to answer since he has been released from the obligation to observe confidentiality about his conversations with his client, which alone would justify the right to remain silent; noting that the right to invoke lawyer-client confidentiality is there to protect both the client and his counsel and to guarantee the untroubled and confidential performance of the counsel's difficult professional task; noting therefore that Paolicelli's declaration is not sufficient to invalidate the above-mentioned right to remain silent, which is also intended to protect the defence counsel; for such reasons the court rejects Avvocato Guerrieri's motion, declares that the witness Macrì has the right to invoke lawyer-client confidentiality regarding all questions pertaining to his relationship with his former client Paolicelli, and stipulates that proceedings continue."

Then he turned to me. I was looking at him and at the

same time observing Macrì's face. He had his old expression back. He was pleased. He must have been thinking that he'd be on his way home in a few minutes.

"Avvocato Guerrieri, you have been informed of the court's decision. If you have no other questions, I mean questions not pertaining to the substance of the conversations between the witness and the defendant, perhaps we could —"

"I accept the court's decision, Your Honour. I only have a few more questions. Obviously on topics not covered by lawyer-client confidentiality."

He looked at me. He was getting impatient and made no attempt to hide the fact. "Go ahead and ask your questions, but please bear in mind that the matter of their relevance will be subject to the most rigorous scrutiny from now on."

"Thank you, Your Honour. Avvocato Macrì, just a few more questions, if you don't mind."

I looked at him before going on. His face was telling me different things. One of these was: Guerrieri, you're a loser. I offered you an opportunity to get out of this mess gracefully, but unfortunately for you you're an idiot. So in a few minutes I'll be walking out of here as cool as a cucumber, and with my money still in my pocket.

"The defendant's wife, Signora Paolicelli, has told us that when the sequestration order on her car was lifted, you personally went and fetched it from the police pound. Can you confirm the circumstances of this for us?"

"Yes. Signora Paolicelli asked me if I'd do this for her as a favour, and as she was alone, and in a difficult situation —"

"Actually, Signora Paolicelli told it rather differently. She said it was you who offered to go and pick up the car."

"I think Signora Paolicelli's memory is at fault. Unless *someone* advised her to remember it that way."

I felt the blood rush to my face, and I had to make an effort not to rise to the bait.

"Very well. We'll take note that you and Signora Paolicelli have given different accounts. Now I'd like to ask you if you know a man named Luca Romanazzi."

He controlled himself, but couldn't help giving a slight start. The question about the car he'd been expecting. This one he hadn't. I had the impression he was doing a quick, nervous mental calculation as to what was the best thing to say. He must have concluded – correctly – that as I had brought up the name Romanazzi I presumably had some evidence that they knew each other, so it would be a stupid idea to deny it.

"Yes, I know him. He's a client of mine."

"Do you mean you've defended him in court?"

"I think so."

"You think so? In which court?"

"What do you mean?"

"Where was the trial? Reggio Calabria, Rome, Bari, Bolzano?"

"I really don't remember . . . And anyway, what has Romanazzi got to do with any of this?"

This was a tricky moment. If Mirenghi intervened now and asked me to explain, then in all likelihood everything would go pear-shaped.

"So you don't recall where it was. Are you sure you defended him in court, or is it possible you merely gave him legal advice on some matter?"

"That's possible."

"I see."

"But I repeat, I'd like to know what Romanazzi has to do with any of this. Apart from anything else, you're asking me questions about my relationship with a client, and I have no intention of answering such questions."

I was about to reply but Mirenghi beat me to it. A few moments earlier, I'd seen Russo whisper something in his ear.

"In point of fact, Avvocato Macrì, it isn't the same thing at all. In this particular case, you are being asked whether or not you know a certain person and under what circumstances. You are not being asked to report anything relating to your professional relationship. There are no grounds for lawyer-client confidentiality. Please answer the question."

"It's possible it wasn't in court."

"You advised him, then?"

"Yes."

"When you still worked in Reggio Calabria?"

"No. I'm sure it was later, in Rome."

"I see. I assume the two of you met in your office."

He made a movement with his head. It could mean yes, but I wanted it to be in the transcript. In the course of a few minutes, Macrì's mood had changed a lot. His troubles weren't over yet. On the contrary.

"Is that a yes?"

"Yes."

"Is it correct to say that you and Signor Romanazzi met only in your office, and only for professional reasons?"

"I can't say for certain that we never bumped into each other outside my office . . ."

"Naturally. Is it correct to say, though, that the relationship between you and Romanazzi was strictly professional?"

And now there were other emotions on his face besides hatred. Including the beginnings of fear. He didn't answer the question, but I didn't mind.

"Could you tell us if Signor Romanazzi has a criminal record?"

"I don't believe he has."

"You don't know if he has ever been charged with cross-border drug trafficking?"

I'd have liked to be able to read his mind, to see what was happening in his head. What frantic acrobatics he was doing to decide how to conduct himself, to figure out what he could deny and what he was obliged to say in order not to run the risk of being proved wrong.

"I think he has been charged with narcotics offences, but has never been sentenced."

His upper lip was covered in small beads of sweat. He was feeling hounded.

"Now I'd like to ask you if you are aware of the fact that Signor Romanazzi was on board the same ferry on which the defendant Paolicelli travelled before he was arrested."

How the hell did I know that?

"I know absolutely nothing about it."

"I see. Have you ever had occasion to spend time with Signor Romanazzi outside your professional relationship? For, shall we say, private reasons?"

"No."

I took a deep breath, before landing the next blow. Always breathe in before hitting hard, and out again once the punch has hit the target.

"Have you and Signor Romanazzi ever travelled together?"

The blow hit him in the solar plexus and took his breath away.

"Travelled together?"

Answering a question with another question is an absolutely

foolproof indicator of a witness being in trouble. It means he's trying to gain time.

"Yes, travelled together."

"I don't think —"

"Have you ever been in Bari with Signor Romanazzi?"

"In Bari?"

Another counter-question, to gain time. Weren't you supposed to be destroying me, you son of a bitch?

"Have you ever stayed at the Hotel Lighthouse with your *client* Luca Romanazzi?"

"I've been in Bari several times, not just when I was defending Paolicelli, and I think I may have stayed at the hotel you mentioned. But not with Romanazzi."

As he finished answering, the raincoat slipped from his arm and fell to the floor. He bent to pick it up and I noticed that his movements weren't as agile as before.

"You know we can easily check the hotel register and find out if your *client*, Signor Romanazzi, spent the night in that hotel at the same time you were there."

"You can check whatever you like. I don't know if Romanazzi was in the hotel when I was there, but we didn't go there together."

He didn't even believe it himself. He was like one of those boxers who keep raising their arms mechanically, driven by nothing but instinct. They're no longer parrying, they're taking punches all over, and they're on the verge of going down.

"Would it surprise you to learn that, not just on one, but on two occasions, you and Signor Romanazzi spent the same night in the same hotel, the Lighthouse?"

"Your Honour" – he had raised his voice, but it wasn't very firm – "I don't know what Avvocato Guerrieri is talking about. I'd really like to know where he got this information from, if it was acquired legally and —"

I interrupted him. "Your Honour, I don't have to tell the court that the defence is allowed to carry out investigations. And this *is* material covered by lawyer-client confidentiality. In any case, to avoid any misunderstandings, the question now is not: *How did Avvocato Guerrieri come by this information?* The question is: *Is this information true or not?*"

I looked Mirenghi in the face, waiting to continue.

"Go on, Avvocato Guerrieri."

"Thank you, Your Honour. So, to sum up: you deny coming to Bari with Signor Romanazzi on two occasions and spending the night, on both occasions, at the Hotel Lighthouse."

"It could have been a coincidence —"

"It could have been a coincidence that on two occasions when you came to Bari and spent the night at the Lighthouse, Signor Romanazzi was also staying there."

It must have sounded ridiculous even to him, hearing it said aloud like that. So he didn't say anything, just held his hands open.

"And can you confirm to us that you didn't know Signor Romanazzi was on board the ferry on which the defendant Paolicelli travelled before he was arrested?"

"I don't know anything about that."

"So you don't know that Signor Romanazzi, on returning from Montenegro, spent the night in Bari, once again – as chance would have it – at the Hotel Lighthouse?"

"I don't know what you're talking about."

I let his last words hang in the air. As if I had been about to ask another question. I kept him dangling for a few seconds, expecting another blow. I savoured the moment, all by myself. Because I knew that the fight was over, but I was the only person in the courtroom who did.

I'll destroy you.

Just try.

I wondered if Natsu was still in the courtroom and had seen it all. I suddenly remembered her perfume and her smooth skin, and it made me feel dizzy.

"Thank you, Your Honour. I have no other questions."

Mirenghi asked the prosecutor if he had any questions for the witness. He said no, thank you, he didn't have any.

"You may go, Avvocato Macrì."

Macrì stood up, said goodbye, and walked out without looking at me. Without looking at anyone.

The atmosphere in the courtroom was electric. There was an energy in the air that you sometimes feel when a hearing comes off its pre-ordained rails and travels to unexpected places. It only happens every now and again, and when it does everyone notices.

Even Russo had noticed, maybe even the assistant prosecutor.

"Are there any other requests, before we declare the hearing closed?"

I got slowly to my feet. "Yes, Your Honour. Following the examination of the witness Macrì, I wish to request that certain documents be admitted in evidence. For reasons I don't think it is necessary to explain, I ask for the admission of Luca Romanazzi's police file, a copy of the passenger list from the ferry on which my client Fabio Paolicelli travelled, and a copy of the register of the Hotel Lighthouse for the years 2002 and 2003."

Mirenghi exchanged a few words with the other two judges. He was speaking under his breath, but I could hear him asking the other two if they should retire to their chamber to come to a decision about my request. I didn't hear what the others said, but they didn't retire. Instead, he dictated a brief ruling in which he accepted my requests and adjourned the hearing for another week, to allow time for those documents to be obtained and for closing arguments to be prepared.

44

That week passed very quickly. Before I knew it, it was nearly over.

The day before the hearing, as I was looking through the papers and trying to jot down an outline of what I was going to say in my closing argument, a strange, incongruous thought came into my head. I had the idea that time was a spring inside me that had been squeezed as far as it would go and was now at last to be released. And it would project me somewhere unknown.

I wondered what this image that had appeared so suddenly, so mysteriously and so vividly in my head could possibly mean, and couldn't find an answer.

At eight o'clock that evening Natsu came to the office. Just a flying visit to say hello and to find out how my preparations for next day were going, she said.

"You look tired. Worn out."

"Do you mean I'm less handsome than usual?"

A not very good attempt to be witty.

"You're even more handsome this way," she replied, seriously. She was about to add something else but then decided it was better not to. "Do you still have a lot of work to do?"

"Yes, I do. We're on a knife-edge. There are several arguments I could use, and the problem is to select the right ones. The ones that will sway the judges. In an appeal like this it's not at all clear what those arguments are."

"What are the possibilities of an acquittal?"

Ah, yes, that was just the question I needed, with my closing argument still to be written, and these incomprehensible, slightly unsettling images popping into my head.

There are cases in which you know for certain that the client will be found guilty, and your work is just a question of damage limitation. There are others in which you know for certain that he will be acquitted however good or bad your work was, and would be acquitted even if he didn't have a lawyer at all. In these cases your job is to make the client believe that acquittal depends on your amazing skills, in order to justify your fee.

In all other cases it's better, much better, not to risk making predictions.

"It's hard to say. The odds certainly aren't on our side."

"Sixty to forty against? Seventy to thirty?"

Let's say ninety to ten. Being optimistic.

"Yes, I'd say seventy to thirty is a realistic forecast."

Maybe she believed me, maybe she didn't. From her face there was no way of knowing.

"May I smoke?"

"Go ahead. But on your way out, tell Maria Teresa it was you. Because of the smell, you know. Ever since I quit, she's been checking up on me like a Salvation Army officer."

She gave a hint of a smile, then lit her cigarette and smoked half of it before she spoke again.

"I often find myself thinking how things might have been for the two of us. If circumstances had been different."

I said nothing, tried to keep my face as expressionless as possible. I don't know if I succeeded, but it was a pointless effort anyway, because she wasn't looking at me. She was looking somewhere inside herself, and outside that room.

"And I often think of that night when you came home with me. When Midori had nightmares and you held her hand. It's strange, you know. When I think of you, that's what I remember most of all. Much more than the times we were together, at your place."

Great. Thanks for telling me that. It does wonders for my male pride.

I didn't say that.

I told her that I often thought of that night, too, but that the other thing I particularly remembered was that Sunday morning in the park. She nodded, as if I had told her something she already knew. Something that neither of us could add anything to.

"I have to ask you another question, Guido, and you must tell me the truth."

I told her to go ahead and ask me the question, thinking as I did so how relative the truth is.

"Is Fabio innocent? Forget about the appeal hearing, the papers, your investigations, your line of defence. I want to know if you're convinced of his innocence. I want to know if he's been telling me the truth."

No, you can't ask me that. I can't answer that question. I don't know. He's probably been telling the truth, but I can't completely rule out the possibility that he was in league with Romanazzi, Macrì and God knows who else in the drugs racket. I can't even rule out the possibility that your husband did even worse things than that, a long time ago when he was a young Fascist.

I should have answered her like that. I should have told her it wasn't part of my job as a lawyer to find out if a client is telling the truth. But there were other things I'd done that weren't part of my job as a lawyer either.

"He's been telling you the truth."

At that precise moment, I saw our paths, which had touched for that brief time, separate and go off in different directions, getting further and further away from each other. A few minutes passed, and neither of us said a word. Maybe she too had had a vision similar to mine, or perhaps she was only thinking about the answer I had given her.

"So I'll see you tomorrow in court?"

"Yes," I replied.

"Tomorrow in court," I said, out loud, once I was alone.

45

The assistant prosecutor that morning was Montaruli.

We'd twice had the worst magistrate in the Department of Public Prosecutions and twice had the best, I thought, without any particular effort at originality.

It should have been a bad sign. If Porcelli, or someone like him, had been there, I wouldn't have worried, even about his closing argument. Some assistant prosecutors stand up when the presiding judge gives them the floor, say, "I ask for the sentence to be upheld," and consider they have earned their salary.

Some even have the nerve to complain that they work too hard.

Tired and disillusioned as Montaruli might be, he wasn't a member of that club. It should have been a bad sign that it was him, but instead I was pleased.

"You've done an excellent job in this case," he said, walking up to my bench.

I stood up.

"I read over the transcripts yesterday," he went on, "and that's what I thought. An excellent job. I'll ask for the sentence to be upheld, but I wanted you to know that I really had to think long and hard about it. Much more than I usually do in cases like this."

As the judges came in, he gave me his hand, and for some reason his grip conveyed a slight sadness, an inscrutable nostalgia. Then he turned and went back to his seat, and so he didn't see the gesture I made, nodding slightly so that my head touched my closed fist. A greeting and a mark of respect, which Margherita had taught me.

Where was she at that moment?

For a few seconds, as I thought about that question, things around me went out of focus and the voices became a blur. By the time I'd come back to my senses, Montaruli had already started speaking.

". . . so we appreciate the efforts made by counsel for the defence. Efforts which have shown a rare degree of commitment, and it is only right to acknowledge them. These rare efforts notwithstanding, no evidence has been produced during this hearing which substantially helps the defendant's case.

"Confronted with one overwhelming piece of evidence – the discovery of drugs in the defendant's private car – counsel for the defence has succeeded only in presenting us with a series of conjectures, insufficient in themselves to invalidate the body of evidence on which the original sentence was based. Needless to say, it is not enough to suggest some vague alternatives to the hypothesis put forward by the prosecution for this hypothesis automatically to fall apart.

"If that were the case, no one would ever be found guilty. It is always possible to formulate hypothetical alternatives to the version of the facts which has led to a defendant being sentenced. For these alternatives to constitute a valid basis for a request for acquittal, let alone an actual acquittal, they must at least be somewhat plausible.

"The higher court of appeal has often stated that what is presented as evidence must allow for the reconstruction of the facts and the guilt or innocence of the defendant in terms that are so certain as to exclude the acceptability of any other reasonable solution. Not to mention more abstract, more remote possibilities, based on conjecture and speculation. Otherwise, it would be sufficient to say to the judge: *Look, things might not have happened the way the prosecution alleges, because everything is possible,* and obtain the defendant's acquittal for that very reason.

"If that were so, it would no longer be a question of presenting evidence, but of making a demonstration *per absurdum* following rules borrowed from the exact sciences, which have no place in the exercise of the law.

"In court, what is evaluated is the acceptability of the hypotheses proposed by the parties to explain the facts of the case. The final decision must rest on the most plausible hypothesis, in other words, the one which can encompass within a coherent, persuasive framework *all* the elements that have emerged from the investigation and the court proceedings.

"In this particular case, none of the new evidence presented by counsel for the defence appears to contradict the hypothesis put forward by the prosecution. On the contrary, it can easily be encompassed by that hypothesis. Let me briefly explain how."

He briefly explained how. Everything he said was sensible and convincing.

For a few minutes, my attention wandered, and I tried to imagine the kind of closing argument another prosecutor might have made. Porcelli, for example. By the time I again focused on Montaruli's words, he was talking about Macrì.

"There can be no doubt that the witness Avvocato Macrì has not conducted himself in a particularly open manner, either in the course of his testimony or indeed in the course of this whole affair.

"Clearly, he has not told the whole truth about his relations with Luca Romanazzi. And it is certainly possible that this Romanazzi is involved in some way in the illegal traffic which forms the basis of this case.

"But none of the new evidence proposed by the defence is incompatible with the charges against the defendant. Let us take it as read that Romanazzi was involved in smuggling the cocaine into the country. In other words, let us take as read something which, although pure conjecture, is reasonable. But even if we do, what of it? Does it rule out Paolicelli's guilt?

"Could not the fact that Paolicelli was defended by the same lawyer as Romanazzi instead constitute a further indication that Paolicelli is part of a highly structured criminal organization, capable, like all such organizations, of providing legal assistance to its members when they are in trouble?

"Let me propose a different hypothesis. Paolicelli and Romanazzi travel together on the ferry, because they are accomplices in the cocaine smuggling operation. Passing through customs, Paolicelli is stopped and the drugs discovered. Romanazzi wants to help him and does it in the only way he can, given the way things are developing. He can hardly launch an attack on the customs police barracks and free his friend. Instead, he sends for a lawyer he trusts, a lawyer whose job it is, according to this hypothesis, to provide legal assistance to any members of the organization who are in trouble with the law."

He stopped for a moment to catch his breath. I don't think it was also to collect his thoughts. His thoughts seemed pretty lucid to me.

"Let me be clear about one thing. I'm not saying it happened

226

like this, because I don't have sufficient evidence to state that categorically. I'm saying it *could* have happened like this. I'm saying it is a reasonable conjecture, which encompasses the new evidence presented by counsel for the defence in the course of this hearing within the original prosecution hypothesis. It is a conjecture at least as reasonable as the one which I am sure counsel for the defence will propose to you in his closing argument.

"But when I say 'at least as reasonable', I am erring on the side of caution. In point of fact, it is a *much* more reasonable conjecture than the hypothesis that there was some kind of conspiracy, some fiendish plot to destroy Paolicelli.

"In conclusion, we have two hypotheses to explain the new evidence presented during this hearing. One, which is fully compatible with the overwhelming body of evidence presented in the original trial, would lead to the sentence being upheld.

"The other, of whose validity counsel for the defence will soon attempt to convince you, is based on a whole series of hypothetical and unlikely conjectures. What is being proposed as grounds for acquittal is not a reasonable doubt but, if you'll pardon the expression, an improbable doubt. A doubt that derives from imagination, not from a strict application of evidential method.

"I am sure that counsel for the defence will be quite capable of presenting this improbable version of events in an appealing and persuasive way. I am also sure, however, that you will keep that rigorous evidential method constantly in mind, because without it there is only chaos.

"It is in the name of that method that I ask you to uphold the original sentence."

46

Slow motion.

One frame at a time.

The prosecutor concludes his closing argument and sits down. Mirenghi tells me that I may proceed with my closing argument. I hesitate for a moment, then slowly stand up. I make my usual gesture of adjusting my robe around my shoulders. Then I straighten the knot in my tie. I pick up a sheet of paper containing my notes. Then I have second thoughts and put it back on the bench along with the other papers. I push my chair back, and move around the bench until I have my back to it.

The judges are there in front of me, looking at me.

I think about a lot of things that have nothing to do with this hearing. Or maybe they do, but in a way that's hard to explain, even to myself.

Whichever way things go, I think, after this case is over I'll be alone. I'll never see that little girl again.

At least, not as a little girl.

It's possible I'll meet her again many years from now, in the street, by chance. I'm sure to recognize her. I'll have white hair – I already have some now – and she will pass me by without even noticing me. Why should she?

Where is Margherita now? What time is it in New York?

Slow motion.

Mirenghi ostentatiously cleared his throat. And all at once

time started moving normally again. The people and objects in the courtroom were once again solid and real.

I glanced at my watch and started to speak.

"Thank you, Your Honour. The assistant prosecutor is right. You must, as you always do, apply strict criteria for evaluating the evidence in order to come to a decision. He is right when he talks, in a *theoretical* way, about method. But now, in a concrete way, dealing with the specific case concerning us today, we must see if it is possible to arrive at an acceptable conclusion with which we can all agree."

I turned back to the bench and again picked up the sheet of paper with my notes.

"The assistant prosecutor, quoting the higher appeal court, said . . . I've noted down his words . . . *the higher court of appeal has often stated that what is presented as evidence must allow for the reconstruction of the facts and the guilt or innocence of the defendant in terms that are so certain as to exclude the acceptability of any other reasonable solution. Not to mention other more abstract, more remote possibilities. Otherwise, it would no longer be a question of presenting evidence, but of making a demonstration* per absurdum *following rules borrowed from the exact sciences, which have no place in the exercise of the law.*

"Correct.

"What that means, basically, is that it is not possible to disprove the validity of the prosecution's hypothesis by presenting other alternatives based on imagination and conjecture. Developing this concept, the assistant prosecutor has asserted that, when faced with an abstract plurality of explanations, we have to choose the one explanation capable of encompassing all the evidence in a coherent way. In other words, leaving aside any improbable or merely conjectural explanations, on the basis – and let us take note of this, because this is where the weakness of the prosecution argument rests – on the basis of a criterion of plausibility that can be expressed in statistical terms, that is, in terms of probability.

"Plausibility, as the assistant prosecutor sees it, means compatibility with a kind of script of normality, developed on the basis of what *usually* happens.

"What usually happens, when certain given elements of fact are present, therefore becomes the criterion according to which we decide what may have happened in a specific case."

All three were listening to me. Incredibly, Russo seemed the most alert.

I went over everything that had emerged during the hearings. It didn't take long. They had already admitted all these things as evidence, they were as familiar with them as I was. This recap was only there to introduce my main argument.

"At the end of the day, what is it that we do in court? All of us, I mean. Policemen, *carabinieri*, prosecutors, defence lawyers, judges? We all tell stories. We take the raw material contained in the evidence, gather it together, and give it a structure and meaning in stories that present a plausible version of past events. The story is acceptable if it explains all the evidence, if it doesn't leave anything out, if it forms a coherent narrative.

"And a coherent narrative depends on the reliability of the laws of experience, which we use to extract from the evidence those stories which present a version of past events.

"Stories that in a way – in an etymological way – we have to *invent*.

"Let us look briefly at the two stories which can be told on the basis of the material that has been presented to us.

"The story told in the sentence handed down in the original trial is a simple one. Paolicelli purchases a large quantity of drugs in Montenegro and tries to smuggle these drugs into the country hidden in his car. He is discovered and arrested. And even confesses his guilt.

"This story is constructed on the basis of a single significant fact: the discovery of the drugs in Paolicelli's car at the border post. To go from an established fact – the presence of drugs in Paolicelli's car – to the unestablished sequence of events which constitute the story told in the sentence from the original trial, it is necessary to go through a logical process.

"How do I know that the story I have told is a true account of past events? By applying to the established fact – the finding of the drugs in Paolicelli's car – a law of experience, which we could summarize like this: if someone has a quantity of drugs in his car, those drugs are his.

"This is a highly reliable law of experience. It tallies with common sense. Normally, if I have something in my car – especially if it's something of great value – then that something belongs to me. It's a law of experience. But it isn't a scientific law, and it *allows for alternatives*.

"The assistant prosecutor says, quite rightly, that the new evidence that has emerged during this appeal hearing is not incompatible with this story."

I glanced at Montaruli before I continued.

"But now let's see what other story it is possible to tell on the basis of the evidence we have.

"A family spends a week's holiday in Montenegro. At night their car stays in the hotel car park and – in case it needs to be moved – the keys are left with the porter. The night before they are due to leave someone takes those keys.

"Someone who knows that Paolicelli and his wife are going back to Italy the next day, in that same car.

"This someone, with his accomplices, strips the bodyshell from Paolicelli's car – his wife's car, to be more precise – and fills it with drugs. Then they put everything back where it was, the car and the keys. It's a good way to carry out an extremely lucrative operation with the minimum of risk. An operation set up by an organized group, which goes about things in a highly professional way, involving a division of roles and tasks. One of these tasks must be to check that everything goes well on the journey, to follow the unwitting courier and make sure the drugs are retrieved once they are in Italy. This retrieval probably to be carried out through a targeted theft of the car itself.

"At the border post in Bari, something goes wrong. The customs police find the drugs and arrest Paolicelli, who makes a confession without a lawyer being present – a confession which is therefore completely unusable – with the sole purpose of avoiding his wife being arrested.

"Immediately after the arrest, someone, in circumstances which are bizarre to say the least, suggests to Paolicelli's wife that she appoint a lawyer from Rome. This lawyer has previously had a nasty brush with the justice system himself, in which he was arrested, charged and then acquitted for the offence of criminal conspiracy to traffic drugs. This same lawyer has a private relationship, the nature of which is unclear, with a man who – as Macrì himself says – has also been charged with drug trafficking. By a curious coincidence, this man was travelling on the same ferry as Paolicelli.

"Of course it could be, as the prosecutor hypothesizes, that Paolicelli and this man were accomplices in the illegal operation.

"I must point out, however, that there exists at least one important piece of evidence which contradicts this hypothesis. The file contains printouts of the defendant's mobile phone records, and those of his wife, during the week immediately prior to the arrest. They were acquired, quite correctly, in an attempt to identify possible accomplices, but when they were examined nothing significant emerged. There weren't many calls that week, almost all of them between Paolicelli and his wife, and none to numbers in Montenegro. And none to any phone users related to Romanazzi. If the customs police had found any, they would surely have highlighted it, given that Romanazzi had previously been charged with drug offences. Instead, the note that was sent to the Prosecutor's Department with these printouts simply states that nothing significant emerged from an examination of the phone records.

"We can therefore explain the presence of Romanazzi on board that ferry by saying that he was there to keep a close watch, without any risk to himself, on the transporting of the drugs by the unwitting Paolicelli, and to make sure that the next phase, the retrieval of the drugs, went well.

"And it could be that it was in fact Romanazzi who suggested to Paolicelli's wife, through a go-between, that she appoint Macrì.

"Why would he do that? To follow as closely as possible, through a person he trusted completely, the development of proceedings. To make sure that Paolicelli didn't tell the investigators anything that might compromise the organization, for example anything about the hotel in Montenegro, the person with whom he left the keys, and so on. Indeed, Macrì advises Paolicelli to exercise his right to remain silent and the whole process goes through without the defendant

233

making a single statement, apart from the false confession he made immediately after the arrest.

"Let us also remember that when the sequestration order on the car is lifted – a car which is the property of Paolicelli's wife – Macrì is anxious to go personally and pick up the car from the police pound.

"What lawyer does something like that? And why does he do it? As a rule, as we all know, the lawyer gets the sequestration order lifted and then the client is the one who goes to pick up the car.

"Macrì acts in a very unusual way, for which we must find a reasonable explanation, even if only a hypothetical one. Isn't it possible that there was something in the car which the investigators had not found and which those responsible for the illegal operation had a major interest in retrieving? More drugs, perhaps. Or else a GPS tracker that had been planted in the car at the same time as the drugs. I'm sure you know what a GPS tracker is."

Of course I was sure they *didn't* know.

"A GPS tracker is a satellite signaller. It's used as an anti-theft device in luxury cars, and is also used by the police to keep track of the cars of suspects under investigation. With a GPS it's possible, from a long distance, to track down the location of a car to within a few yards. And it's all done using mobile phone networks. If the device installed in the car is found, then it's possible to trace those phones. Do I need to add anything more? Is it really absurd to hypothesize that the gang which planted the drugs in Paolicelli's car also installed a GPS tracker to be on the safe side, and the customs police did not find it? Is it absurd to hypothesize that Macrì personally collected the car in order to retrieve any remaining drugs and that compromising device? That device which, if found by the investigators, would have made it possible for the police to trace the traffickers' phones? How else can we explain the actions of a lawyer who not only gets the sequestration order lifted, which is perfectly normal, but also goes personally to collect the car, which is quite abnormal?"

At this point I had to resist the impulse to turn round and see who was still in the courtroom. To check if there were any unknown or suspicious-looking faces. Anyone sent by Macrì to keep an eye on what I was saying, to see just how stupid I'd been and how great a risk I liked to take. To anyone listening, it must have seemed a purely technical pause, the kind you use to keep people's attention.

Obviously, I didn't turn round. But when I resumed, I still felt an unpleasant undercurrent, a sense of unease. A creeping fear.

"Is it a fanciful story? Perhaps, in the sense that it's the result of a series of reasonable hypotheses. Is it an absurd story? Certainly not. Above all, it is a story which – at least as far as the transporting of drugs in the ways we are hypothesizing is concerned – has already been told in the past, in other investigations. There have been other cases in which our investigators and those of other countries have discovered similar illegal operations involving the transporting of narcotics by the same means.

"It could be objected: *That's what* you *say, Guerrieri.*

"It's true, it is what I say, but, if you have any doubts about the existence of such a modus operandi, you still have time, even after you retire to deliberate, to arrange for further evidence to be admitted, for example a statement by the head of the narcotics section of the Bari Flying Squad, or any other officer in a narcotics unit, who will be able to confirm that this particular criminal practice has indeed been known to take place."

It was at this point that I glanced at my watch and realized that I had been speaking for an hour. Too long.

I could see from their faces that they were still following me, but I wouldn't be able to keep their attention much longer. I had to try and bring my speech to a conclusion. I quickly returned to more general topics: the question of method, my interpretation of the evidence as opposed to the assistant prosecutor's.

"Whenever it is possible to construct a *multiplicity of stories* capable of encompassing all the evidence within a coherent narrative, we must conclude that the evidence is doubtful, that there is no legal certainty, and that therefore we must acquit.

"Needless to say, in this area it is not a question of a competition between the degrees of probability of the various stories. To put it another way: it is not enough for the assistant prosecutor to propose a *more* probable story to win the case.

"In order to win the case, in other words, to make sure that the sentence is upheld, the assistant prosecutor must propose the *only* acceptable story. In other words, the only acceptable explanation of the facts of the case. All the defence has to do is propose a possible explanation.

"I repeat: this is not a contest between degrees of probability. I know perfectly well that the assistant prosecutor's story is more probable than mine. I know perfectly well that the law of experience on which the assistant prosecutor's story is based is stronger than mine. But this law of experience is not life. It is, like all laws of experience, *a way of interpreting the facts of life*, an attempt to make sense of them. But life, especially those areas of life which result in legal proceedings, is more complicated than our attempts to reduce it to classifiable rules and to well-ordered, coherent stories.

"A philosopher has said that facts and actions have no meaning in themselves. The only thing that can mean anything is the narrative we make out of those facts and actions.

"We all of us – and not only in court – construct stories to give meaning to facts which in themselves have none. To try and bring order out of chaos.

"When we get down to it, stories are all that we have."

I stopped. A thought had suddenly crossed my mind. Who was I saying these things to? Who was I really talking to?

Was I talking to the judges in front of me? Or to Natsu, who was behind me even though I couldn't see her? Or Paolicelli, who – however things ended up – would never know the meaning of this story? Or was I talking to myself and was everything else – *everything* else – just a pretext?

For a few moments, I thought I knew what it all meant, and I gave a slight, melancholy smile. Just for a few moments. Then that meaning, if I really had found one, disappeared.

I told myself that I had to start speaking again, had to bring my argument to a conclusion. But I didn't know what else to say. Or rather, I didn't feel like saying anything. All I wanted was to get out of there.

Still I didn't speak. I saw a questioning look on the faces of the judges. They were starting to get impatient.

I had to bring my argument to a conclusion.

"Life does not work by selecting the likeliest, most believable or most well-ordered stories. Life isn't well ordered and doesn't always tally with the laws of experience. In life there are sudden strokes of good luck and bad luck. You may win the lottery; you may contract a rare, fatal disease.

"Or you may be arrested for something you didn't do."

I took a deep breath. I felt as if all the exhaustion in the world had descended on my shoulders.

"The assistant prosecutor and I have told you many things. The kind of things that help us to debate cases and to come to conclusions. The kind of things that help us to justify our arguments and our decisions, to give us the illusion that they are rational arguments and decisions. Sometimes they are, sometimes they aren't, but that's not really the most important thing. The most important thing is that at the moment of making the decision you are – *we are* – alone, faced with the question: am I sure this man is guilty?

"We are alone, faced with the question: what is the right thing to do? Not in the abstract, not according to any method or theory, but specifically, in *this* case, in relation to the life of *this* man."

I had said these last words almost under my breath. I stood there in silence. Pursuing a thought, I think. Perhaps searching for a closing phrase. Or perhaps searching for the meaning of what I had said, and leaving the words to hang in the air.

"Have you finished, Avvocato Guerrieri?" Mirenghi's tone was polite, almost cautious. As if he had realized something and didn't want to appear intrusive or tactless.

"Thank you, Your Honour. Yes, I've finished."

He then turned to Paolicelli, who was standing there with his hands together, his head against the bars.

He asked him if he had anything he would like to say before the court retired to deliberate. Paolicelli turned to me, then back to the judges. He seemed to be about to say something. In the end he just shook his head and said no, thank you, Your Honour, he had nothing to say.

It was at that moment, as the judges gathered their papers to retire to their chamber, that I was struck by a feeling that I was hovering between dream and reality.

Had the events of the past four months really happened? Had Natsu and I really made love, twice, in my apartment? Had I walked in the park with Natsu and little Midori, taking unfair advantage of those few minutes to play father, or had I only imagined it? And was the defendant Fabio Paolicelli really the Fabio Rayban I'd been obsessed with during my teenage years? And did it still matter to me to find out the truth about that distant past, supposing there had ever been a truth to find out? On what basis can we say with any certainty that an image in our head is the result of something we've actually seen or an act of the imagination? What *really* distinguishes our dreams from our memories?

It lasted a few seconds. When the judges disappeared into their chamber my thoughts went back to normal.

Whatever the word means.

47

That day there were several hearings involving prisoners, in various courtrooms, and not many guards. So the head of the escort had asked Mirenghi for permission to take Paolicelli back down to the holding cells so that he could use his men in other courtrooms. When the judges were ready to give their decision, the clerk of the court would call the head of the escort and Paolicelli would be brought back up to the courtroom for the ruling to be read out.

Only Natsu and I were left in the courtroom. We sat down behind the prosecution bench.

"How's Midori?"

She shrugged, a forced smile on her lips. "Well. Quite well. She had a nightmare last night, but it didn't last long. They've become shorter and less violent lately."

We looked at each other for a few moments and then she stroked my hand. Longer than was advisable, if we wanted to be careful.

"Congratulations. It wasn't an easy speech, but I understood everything. You're very good." She hesitated for a moment. "I didn't think you would go to so much trouble."

It was my turn to give a forced smile.

"What's going to happen?"

"Impossible to predict. Or at least I can't. Anything can happen."

She nodded. She hadn't really expected any other answer.

"Can we get out of here, go for a coffee or something?"

"Of course; it'll be a while before the decision."

I was about to add that if they came to a decision straight away it wasn't a good sign. It meant that they had upheld the sentence without even taking into account the things I'd been trying to say. But I stopped myself. It was pointless information, at this stage.

We left the courthouse, had a coffee, then had a little stroll and went back. We didn't talk much. Just enough to give a bit of direction to the silence. I don't know what she was feeling. She didn't tell me and I couldn't figure it out. Or maybe I didn't want to. I felt great tenderness for her, but it was a sad, resigned, distant, intangible tenderness.

At five, the courthouse emptied. Doors closing, voices, hurried footsteps.

And then silence, the strange, unmistakable silence of deserted offices.

It was just before six that we saw the escort coming back into the courtroom with Paolicelli. They passed close to us. He looked at me, searching for a message in my eyes. He didn't find one. In all my years as a lawyer, I've rarely felt so unsure of the result of a case, so incapable of making predictions.

I went back to my seat, while the guards put Paolicelli back in the cage, the prosecutor came back into the courtroom, and Natsu returned to the now deserted public benches.

Then the judges came out, without even ringing the bell.

Mirenghi read out the decision quickly. Before I'd even had time to adjust the robe on my shoulders. He read it with a very tense expression on his face, and I was sure that they hadn't been unanimous. I was sure that Mirenghi had fought for the sentence to be upheld, but that the other two had outvoted him.

The court overturned the previous sentence and acquitted Fabio Paolicelli of the charge against him on the grounds that *the act does not constitute an offence.*

In our jargon the expression *the act does not constitute an offence* can mean many different things. In this case it meant that Paolicelli had indeed physically transported the drugs – that was a fact, there was no doubt – but without being aware of it. There was no motive, and an absence of criminal intent.

The act does not constitute an offence.

Acquittal.

Immediate release of the defendant if not held for other reasons.

Mirenghi caught his breath for a moment and then resumed reading. There was something else.

"The court asks that the ruling and the transcripts of the appeal hearing be sent to the regional anti-Mafia department for examination."

That meant the affair wasn't over. It meant that the anti-Mafia department would deal with my colleague Macrì and his friend Romanazzi.

It might mean trouble for me. But I didn't want to think about that now.

Mirenghi declared the hearing over and turned to leave. Girardi also turned.

But Russo hesitated for a moment. He looked at me and I looked at him. His back was straight and he seemed ten years younger. I'd never seen him like that before. He nodded, almost imperceptibly.

Then he, too, turned and followed the others into the chamber.

48

They let Paolicelli out of the cage. He still had to be taken back to prison to go through the formalities of release, but they didn't put his handcuffs on, because he was a free man now. He came towards me, surrounded by the guards. When he came level with me, he embraced me.

I responded graciously to the embrace, patting him on the back and hoping it would soon be over. After me, he embraced his wife, kissed her on the mouth, and told her he would see her at home that evening.

She said she would come and pick him up but he said no, he didn't want her to.

He didn't want her to go near *that place* even for a moment. He would come home alone, on foot.

He wanted to prepare himself for seeing his daughter, and a walk would be the ideal way of doing that.

Besides, it was spring. It was a nice thing to walk home, free, in the spring.

His lower lip was trembling and his eyes watery, but he didn't cry. At least not while he was still in the courtroom.

Then the head of the escort told him, gently, that they had to go.

One of the guards, a tough-looking old character with very blue eyes and a scar that started under his nose and went across his lips all the way down to his chin, came up to me. He had a voice roughened by cigarettes and thirty years spent among thieves, dealers, traffickers and murderers. He was a prisoner, too, who wouldn't finish his sentence until the day he retired.

"Congratulations, Avvocato. I listened to you and understood everything." He pointed to Paolicelli, who was already walking away with the other two guards. "You saved that man."

And then he rushed off to join his colleagues.

Again, Natsu and I were alone. For the last time.

"And now?"

"Goodbye," I said.

It came out well, I think. Goodbye is a hard word to say. You always run the risk of sounding pathetic, but this time I hit the right note.

She looked at me for a long time. If I let her image go slightly out of focus and replaced her eyes with two big blue circles, I could see her daughter Midori as she would be in twenty years' time.

In 2025. I tried not to think about how old I would be in 2025.

"I don't think I'll ever meet anyone else like you."

"Well, I should hope not," I said. It was meant as a kind of joke, but she didn't laugh.

Instead, she looked around, and when she was sure the courtroom was really deserted, she gave me a kiss.

A real kiss, I mean.

"Goodbye," she said and walked out into the deserted corridor.

I gave her five minutes' head start and then left.

49

All the windows in my apartment were open, but the sounds coming in from the street were curiously muffled. They were like sounds I used to hear many years ago, when I was a child and we went to the park on May afternoons to play football.

I put on a CD, and it wasn't until I'd already played several songs that I realized it was the same one I'd played that first night Natsu had come home with me.

These days miracles don't come falling from the sky.

As I listened to the music, I poured myself a whisky on the rocks, and drank it, and ate corn chips and pistachio nuts. Then I had a long shower in cold water. Without drying myself, I walked round the apartment enjoying the smell of the bath foam on my skin, the music, the slight dizziness I felt because of the whisky, the cool breeze that came in through the open windows and made me shiver.

Once I was dry I got dressed, put on some pointless scent, and went out.

It was mild in the streets. I decided that before having dinner I would walk as far as the Piazza Garibaldi, where my parents and I used to live when I was a child.

When I got there, I was seized with the kind of intangible, all-consuming joy you feel sometimes when you're sucked back into the past. The gardens of the Piazza Garibaldi, that late afternoon in May, looked the way they had all those years ago, and in among the boys playing football were the ghosts of myself and my friends as children, in short trousers and braces, licking the Super Santos ball we'd all chipped in to buy.

I sat down on a bench and sat there looking at the dogs and children and old people until it was dark and almost everyone had gone. Then I left, too, to look for somewhere to eat. I was heading in the direction of the seafront when my phone rang. A private number, the screen said.

"Hello."

"You did it. I really wouldn't have bet on it this time."

I didn't recognize Tancredi's voice immediately, so it took me a couple of seconds to reply.

"Who told you?"

"What's the matter, friend? Don't you know who I am? I'm the police, I know everything that happens in this town. Sometimes I know about it before it even happens."

As Tancredi spoke, it occurred to me that I didn't really feel like walking around, having dinner, maybe getting drunk alone.

"Are you still in your office?"

"Yes. But I think I'm going to shut up shop now and go."

"Do you fancy having dinner together? I'm paying."

He said he'd like that and we arranged to meet in half an hour in the Piazza del Ferrarese, at the start of the old city wall.

We were both punctual, and arrived at the same time from different directions.

"So you were right. I really must congratulate you."

"You knew perfectly well I was right, otherwise you wouldn't have helped me. And if you hadn't helped me I wouldn't have got anywhere."

He was about to say something, but then probably thought he didn't have a witty enough remark. So he shrugged and we started walking.

"The judges have asked for the documents to be sent to the regional anti-Mafia department. In connection with Macrì and Romanazzi, obviously. As of tomorrow I'm asking for a permit to carry a gun."

"You won't need it."

"Of course I'll need it. They'll want someone to pay for this, and I'm top of their list."

"I tell you you won't need it. Romanazzi, Macrì, his driver and their friends will soon have other things to worry about."

"Such as?"

"Such as the fact that they'll be going on holiday at the State's expense in a few weeks' time. A long holiday, I suspect."

"You're arresting them." Congratulations, Guerrieri, I told myself as I said these words. That was a brilliant deduction.

"The investigation isn't based in Bari, so we won't be arresting them ourselves. Someone else will do it. People a lot nastier than us. And I'd say that's enough professional secrets I've given away for today. Let's change the subject; it's time we had something to eat."

We went to a restaurant facing the harbour. It belonged to a client of mine, Tommaso, known as Tommy. Someone I'd helped out of a tight spot a few years earlier. I told Tommy we wanted to sit outside and didn't feel like ordering. Leave it to him, he'd see to everything, he replied as I'd expected him to.

He brought us raw seafood and grilled fish, followed by cream desserts made by his mother, who'd been a cook for forty years. We drank two carafes of white wine. At the end of the meal one of the waiters brought a bottle of ice-cold lemon liqueur. Carmelo lit his cigar. Damn it, I thought, I'm going to smoke a bloody cigarette. So I called Tommaso and asked him to fetch me a Marlboro. He came back a minute later, with a new packet and a lighter. He put both of them down on the table and turned to go.

"No, Tommy," I said, pushing the packet away. "I don't want all of it."

He insisted, saying I might feel like smoking another one later. I was *sure* I'd feel like smoking another one later. And then another, and another. That was why it was better I didn't keep the packet.

"Thanks, Tommy. One's enough."

I lit the cigarette, smoked it in silence, and then asked Tancredi if he wanted to hear a story. He didn't ask any questions. He poured himself a little more liqueur and gestured with his hand for me to begin. I told him everything, from that afternoon in September until the final act, which had taken place a few hours earlier.

By the time I'd finished, the waiters were putting the upturned chairs on the tables and we were the only people left in the place. Although we both had work the next morning, we decided to have a walk along the deserted seafront.

"Carmelo?" I said after walking for about ten minutes in silence.

"Yes?"

"Do you remember *Casablanca*?"

"You mean the film?"

"Yes."

"Of course I remember it."

"Do you remember the last line?"

248

"No. I remember the scene very well, but not the line."

"*Louis, this could be the beginning of a beautiful friendship.* That's how it goes."

He stopped. For a few moments, he stood there, lost in thought, as if trying to grasp the exact meaning of what I had said, so that he could answer appropriately. In the end, though, he just nodded, without looking at me.

I nodded too, and then we carried on walking, side by side, without saying anything more, to the city limits.

Where the houses and restaurants and signs come to an end, and all that's left are the cast-iron lamp-posts and their friendly but mysterious lights.